THE DESTINED

GLENN EIDSON *and* BRENT HURST

iUniverse

THE DESTINED

iUniverse books may be ordered through booksellers or by contacting:

iUniverse
1663 Liberty Drive
Bloomington, IN 47403
www.iuniverse.com
1-800-Authors (1-800-288-4677)

ISBN: 978-1-4917-5645-4 (sc)
ISBN: 978-1-4917-5646-1 (hc)
ISBN: 978-1-4917-5644-7 (e)

Library of Congress Control Number: 2015900651

Printed in the United States of America.

iUniverse rev. date: 1/19/2015

We would like to thank our Lord Jesus Christ and our God in Heaven for giving us this talent and ability. We would also like to thank our families for putting up with us during the past five years while we labored on this endeavor. This work could not have been completed without their support. We hope you, as a reader of science fiction, enjoy this book.

Glenn Eidson and Brent Hurst

CHAPTER 1

Dega Talladega, a blonde, tanned man with a muscular six-foot frame, walked into the library of the university he was attending in southern Florida. He was a student majoring in health and physical education, and so it hadn't been the norm for him to need the library for the classes he'd taken thus far, but the English class he'd just started made it necessary.

He nodded to the lady at the desk as he walked through the doors and scanned the shelves for something that might be relevant to his paper on ancient legends. Written on the far-left shelf toward the back was the word "Occult," which seemed promising, so he began navigating the maze of other students between himself and the occult section. But when he neared it, he became lightheaded, almost to the point of falling. He steadied himself against the bookcase nearest him until the lightheadedness dissipated enough to allow him to walk, and then he turned to leave the building. Then the feeling vanished. He thought it strange but decided that since he was well and already in the library, he might as well find a few books. He turned toward his original destination and began walking

1

again. There was no more lightheadedness, but his heart rate increased somewhat; he automatically attributed it to the worry that something else might happen and thought no more of it.

He reached the section and began thumbing through a short book, entitled *Powers of the Power Holders*. He could immediately tell it wasn't an occult book and that it had been misplaced in the library, but the contents did involve an ancient legend, so he checked out the book and returned to his dorm room to begin his essay. His roommates were all out of town, leaving him peace to work. He began to read.

The book spoke of powers that, every seven hundred years or so, would manifest themselves in humans whom the powers—who could apparently think for themselves—deemed pure enough to become *power holders* and wield the very essence of water, fire, air, earth, lightning, and spirit. The power holders always worked against whatever destructive force was endangering the world, and, upon the accomplishment of this feat, the powers would take their leave of the mortals.

Not much more information was given in the book, so he got on the Internet and did a search on the topic.

The web page loaded and as he read, his pupils began to dilate, he started twitching, and his head started swaying uncontrollably; he thought he was having a seizure but realized that he was thinking too clearly for that. Still unable to control his body, he noticed that his eyes were reading much more quickly than usual and that he was somehow processing all of the information in front of him. His hands moved the mouse to different sites with ease and then opened his word processor. His fingers typed nonstop for a few hours, but it only seemed to him like a few minutes. Suddenly his fingers stopped and he blacked out.

Dega's eyes opened some time later, and he found himself staring at a somehow perfectly written paper. He tried to think of a word to describe how confused he felt but arrived at the conclusion that the English lexicon was insufficient. He had no idea what to do—going to the emergency room wasn't an option; he felt perfectly normal and would have no symptoms to offer except what had just happened, the telling of which he was sure would make the doctors think him insane. He decided to sleep on it and decide the next day how to proceed.

Dega slept deeply and dreamed that dark shadows were assailing him. He could feel the very essences of their beings—war, pestilence, hate, and death—beating on him and shielded himself with his arms.

Dega woke early Sunday morning to dampness in his T-shirt. He reached to move his sheets from him but stopped as he cried out in pain. Both of his arms were very sore, but on his right forearm there was a pain so sharp he couldn't move it. Instinctively, his left hand went to the bruise on his right forearm; the pain intensified momentarily, and he cried out again, but then it began to lessen. A few seconds later, it was completely gone. Dega marveled at this and, out of curiosity, touched his hand to the scar he had on his knee from the time he fell during a hiking trip with friends. Almost immediately, it disappeared. Amazed, he eventually cleansed his skin of all the scars from his youth; his skin looked like it had when he was born: soft, smooth, and scar-free.

Of the two recent curious events—the attacks of the day before and his newfound ability to heal himself—he decided that, since being able to heal himself was obviously a good thing, the attacks were of more importance. He went to the library and got a book on epilepsy—just to be sure he hadn't been too rash to rule it out—and went to the park to read. For an hour he did so without any affirmation that he could be epileptic.

Just when the tedious tone of the book was about to put him to sleep, a boy who looked about six years old ran up to him. "Can you get my kite?" he asked Dega.

"Sure," Dega told him kindly, glad for an escape from his dreadful read. "Where is it?"

The boy pointed at a tree not far off, and he and Dega made their way there. The kite was a fair distance up, caught where the branches were weak, but climbing was the only way to get it down, so he began the ascent. The lower branches held his weight without trouble, but as he neared the kite he found himself staying as close to the trunk as possible, hoping the thick parts of the branches would be his saving grace.

It soon wasn't enough, though; he tested the next branch and found it so flimsy that he decided to go back down, but as he brought his test-foot back onto the branch he was balancing on, his weight became too great and the branch broke, sending him sprawling to the ground. The moment he landed, he felt an excruciating pain in his arm and knew that he had broken it. He screamed and reached with his good hand to his bad arm, and suddenly the pain ceased.

Dega stood, confused and still breathless from screaming. He tested the arm and found it completely whole. He looked around for the boy, who had probably run off from fright, and found several people staring at him. It was obvious that he needed to figure some things out without too many questions, so he nodded to the ones nearest him, retrieved his book, and returned to his dorm.

He sat on his bed and put his head in his hands, trying to make sense of all that had transpired over the past twenty-four hours. Absolutely no explanation came to mind, so he let his mind flow to try to relieve some of the stress that was building within him. His thoughts eventually moved to school, and he began thinking about what he had written in his essay, wondering if he had enough information.

He turned his head to face his computer with the realization that he didn't remember a word he had written.

He practically jumped from the bed into his desk chair. The computer seemed to take years to load, but eventually it did, and he opened the file and began reading in the middle of the essay.

> "Power Holders," as they are referred to in the aforementioned book, is a decent name, though not wholly accurate; they are more than just "Holders." They are the ones chosen by the Powers. They are the ones who wield the Powers. The most accurate name for them is "Destined," as it sums up the basis of their very beings.

Dega found what he was reading uninteresting and skipped a few paragraphs.

> Though these five do have their merits, perhaps the most useful Power is that which is not, we assume, of the natural world: Spirit. Its main functions include mind-reading—though there is disagreement over whether communicating telepathically is included—and healing.

Dega sat back in his chair, stunned. As he considered every-thing he had recently experienced, he realized that the boy at the park had not actually voiced his plea to Dega; he had been about to, but Dega answered before he asked.

Dega's eyes bore into the computer screen before him, though he saw no words.

He knew he was one of his generation's *Destined*.

A black SUV slowed as it reached the uninviting and rugged building known as Hickory Haven Orphanage. The ivy on all sides of the old edifice was ever-growing; the bricks seemed old and brittle. The windows seemed to have a yellow tint, though upon further inspection one could see the age and mistreatment that gave them the hue. The old, wilted trees in the lawn didn't lessen the intimidation.

One of the doors of the SUV opened, and a blonde girl with a small frame and a scruffy, belligerent face stepped out. She held her head high, not ashamed to put her arrogance on full display. One look would let anyone know that her personality wasn't as kind as one would like in a friend.

She could be forgiven, though, for her attitude; she had no parents. Right after she was born, they had carelessly dropped her off and left to live a carefree life; stubborn nuns from past orphanages had been the only parental figures available to her. While the nuns' intolerance had caused her belligerence, her arrogance was just natural.

A slightly obese nun stood by the entrance and waited while the girl strutted along the sidewalk to her. The girl glared at her as if the nun were her worst enemy—which she soon would be, just like the rest of the nuns.

"Drusilla Raelyn." The nun spoke with a soft, quiet, and comforting tone, but it didn't comfort Drusilla; it caused her to hate the orphanage more. She knew the nun's attitude would change upon entering the building. "Welcome."

"My name is not Drusilla." The girl's voice was bitter and cold. "It's *Dru*." Dru's tolerance for the nuns had lessened each time she was shuttled from one orphanage to another.

"Drusilla is the name your parents gave you, so that's what we will call you." The nun's voice was still soft and sweet, but Dru detected a slight smart-aleck tone mixed in with the innocence.

Dru clenched her open hands into fists, which tightened more at every word spoken by the nun, and her normally blue eyes turned to a green hue with her anger. It eventually became clear to the nun that Dru didn't care what she was saying, and she allowed the girl entrance.

The building's age was even more obvious on the inside. The yellow tiles seemed like they originally had been white, the paint that covered the walls was chipped, and there were stains everywhere from spills that the nuns had been too lazy to clean. Hickory Haven was easily the worst orphanage in which Dru had ever had the displeasure to reside.

The two of them entered a room lined with beds. The dormitory was large and swarming with other girls Dru's age, but her attitude made her automatically disrespect them. She would definitely hate it here. She entered the room with fists still clenched, a smirk on her face, and a *don't touch me* look in her eyes and walked toward the only vacant bed. Its sheets seemed like they hadn't been washed in years.

Immediately Dru was bombarded by girls trying to befriend her, but Dru knew it would never happen; she wanted to be alone for the rest of her time there. She had no need for the dejected lowlifes that roamed the depressing halls of Hickory

Haven. In time, the *natives*, as Dru called them, learned to stay away from her, granting Dru her wish of being alone. It was the only thing that made her happy during her entire stay.

Years before, when Dru was five years old, she was sitting in her room alone, in trouble for picking on another kid. While she sat in isolation, her temper began to flare much more than it should have for one so young. Her fists clenched.

Suddenly the anger inside her was too much and had to come out, choosing to take the form of a flame engulfing her hands. She had burned herself before, so at first she was frightened of the fire, but after a few seconds she realized that, even though it clung so strongly to her skin, she couldn't even feel it. She liked what happened, and so of course she didn't tell the nuns because she knew they would make her stop. Eventually, keeping it a secret developed into a habit, and habit was her only motivation until the day she was old enough to realize that what she was able to do should not be possible. Instinct told her that if others knew, she would die, and so she told no one.

Six months passed at Hickory Haven without change, and Dru was more tired of it than she had been the day she arrived. She lay on her old bed alone, once more being punished for bullying another girl. She thought about the first time she had done her "trick." She concentrated and a flame appeared—after so many years, she had perfected being able to create the fire without being angry—which she let move about her hand like a dog in a new yard until it settled above her index finger like a candle.

8

A knock at the door caused her to lose concentration and the flame disappeared. The door opened, and in walked the nun who had greeted her on the doorsteps six months earlier.

"Drusilla, there's someone here to see you, dear."

As had become her custom, Dru glared at the nun and clenched her fists. "I told you, my name is not *Drusilla*; it's *Dru*."

"And *I* told *you*, dear, I will call you by your God-given name." The nun's smart-aleck tone was back. "This way, please."

Dru and the nun navigated a maze of hallways and came to a door through which Dru had never entered. The door opened, and Dru saw a large table with one chair on Dru's side and two more on the other, behind which another door stood.

"Awesome," Dru said sarcastically. "I take it this is to talk about how I treat the other girls again?"

"No, Drusilla," the nun told her, obviously struggling to keep her composure. "We probably *should* discuss your misbehavior, but I have something else to tell you: you've been adopted!" The nun's voice seemed to turn legitimately heart-warming. "Your new parents are about to come in and meet you. I pray you have a wonderful life with your new family."

Dru sighed as she her let stress leave and elation enter. All of the hate that had solidified itself was momentarily forgotten in the exuberance she felt for getting to leave such a horrid place. The people who would take her weren't her real parents, of course, but she decided to take the best thing she could get and accept her adoptive parents.

The door Dru was facing opened, and a married couple walked in. The woman looked to be about five-foot-six and had long brown hair; she entered strutting like an adult version of Dru. Her husband was much taller than she and had black hair. The two sat in the empty chairs and smiled at their adopted child.

The man spoke first. "Hi, Drusilla—"

"Dru," Dru interjected.

The man shrugged. "Okay, we'll call you however you like." Dru had no interest in the rest of the conversation and remained silent through the paper-signing.

Her silence continued in the car on the way to her new home. Her ears, however, perked up when her adoptive parents began talking about how much better the rest of the community would now view them. Never having been one to care about how others saw her, Dru found it interesting to hear her new parents discussing the matter.

Dru's first day at Wright Brothers High School in Miami, Ohio was a relief to her, as it represented seven hours of reprieve from her terrible adoptive parents. She made only one friend, but that was her nature, so she coped. She was honestly somewhat surprised that she made any, but she and Kandi Jenkins—a five-foot-nine brunette with brown eyes and an athletic physique—were a good match, and they had most of their classes together.

Dru admired only one of the sophomore-level teachers; she was fond of the strict disciplinary tactics of her physical education teacher, Mr. Talladega. He, like Dru, was unwilling to put up with nonsense from his students, and so a feeling of gratitude arose in Dru; none of her other teachers cared about what their students did.

One Wednesday after class, Mr. Talladega walked up to Dru as she was leaving the gym. "Do you have a minute?" he asked her.

"If you write me an excuse," she responded.

Mr. Talladega was amused. He breathed, trying to decide

how to start the conversation. "You're unique. I've known that since your first day here. You're a lot more mature than most of your classmates, and all the teachers admire that, but I have to ask: is something bothering you?"

"I'm adopted," Dru answered. She had assumed the reason for her displeasure was obvious.

"But aside from that?" Mr. Talladega continued. "You just don't act like that's all there is."

Dru realized that he could be talking about her *ability*, and she didn't want to go there. "No, nothing else. The food here is worse than what the nuns used to cook."

Mr. Talladega laughed. "I can see that." He stopped smiling and looked at her. "Please don't lie to me. It's the *fire* that's bothering you, isn't it?"

At the word "fire" Dru stiffened. "Did my house burn down or something?" she asked, trying to sound surprised.

"Let me be more specific: you don't understand your ability to make fire." Dru was silent. "Don't act like you don't know what I'm talking about," he continued.

Dru eyed him suspiciously. "Why do you care?"

"Because I'm that way, too. I can't control fire or anything; my power is spirit."

"Spirit?" Dru asked, cracking a smirk. "Like a cheerleader?"

Mr. Talladega laughed again. "No, spirit like …" He stopped to collect his thoughts. "Do you have a cut or anything on your arm?"

Dru was hesitant but pulled up her sleeve, exposing a scar she had gotten years ago in one of her orphanages. Mr. Talladega reached toward her scar but stopped short when she seemed hesitant. "Just give me a second," he said. She nodded, and he touched his fingers to her scar. It disappeared as if it had never been there.

Dru looked at her teacher with amazement. "What *are* we?" she asked him quietly.

"I'll end class early tomorrow and explain more to you; you need to get to your next class right now."

"Can Kandi be here when you do?" Dru asked as he handed her an excuse for being tardy.

"Does she know?" he asked, surprised.

"I didn't see a problem with telling her."

Mr. Talladega considered this. "She's responsible, and if she already knows, I don't see a problem with her coming."

As promised, Mr. Talladega ended class early the next day and explained to them what he had discovered during his study of the topic. "You don't fully believe me yet," he said to them when he was through. "I guess I expected that. Just give it some time and think it through."

Dru hesitated before she voiced her question. "If we eventually did believe you, what are we supposed to be doing?"

Dega answered her simply. "Waiting for the other four to show themselves," he answered.

CHAPTER 2

The friendship between Dru and Kandi grew steadily. By the end of the school year they had become closer than sisters, and it surprised no one when they planned a vacation together. Dega suggested Miami—he told them he kept a summer job there as a lifeguard—and they finalized their plans.

They arrived at their hotel mid-June and, after resting for a few hours, went to the beach. The horizon was gorgeous and the sky filled with birds. They found Dega just where he had said he'd be, resting in his lifeguard chair. "Mr. Talladega!" Kandi called up to him.

Dega looked down. "Hey!" he called back. "You guys made it!"

"Yeah. I'm enjoying not having to go to school," Dru told him.

"Well, I'm technically not supposed to talk to people," Dega said, "so just enjoy yourselves."

"We will!" Kandi cried excitedly. "Thanks!"

The girls left and found an open spot on the white sand to lay their towels down. "This weather's seriously amazing," Kandi said as she flattened the towel in front of her. "Not too hot, and there's a nice breeze."

"Yeah," Dru agreed. Her voice was calm, which Kandi found

an odd reaction from someone who had never been to the beach, but, knowing Dru, she went along with it.

For over an hour the two of them lay there, only thinking about the warm rays on their skin until they heard the beginnings of commotion down the shoreline. Kandi, curious, raised her head to see what was happening. Four people were together where the ocean met the sand, all of them staring out into the water at a form that Kandi couldn't quite make out. "What's *that*, Dru?"

Dru lazily raised her head. "Can't tell. Almost looks like somebody having trouble staying above the water." Dru noticed Kandi move. "Don't bother going out there; he probably just wants attention."

"He doesn't look like he's acting," Kandi said. She stood and started toward the watching assembly.

"They've got lifeguards out here for a reason," Dru protested sleepily. "Don't worry yourself."

Kandi arrived quickly at the spot where the other beachgoers were congregating, from where she could clearly see that it was indeed a boy struggling to swim. "Has somebody gone out there to help him yet?" Kandi asked to no one in particular.

An older man closest to her answered. "The waves are a lot stronger today than they usually are; none of us can handle them. Susan went to get a lifeguard, though."

Kandi looked at the waves and didn't find them too terribly intimidating, so she raced out toward the boy. She had underestimated the ocean's strength, but it wasn't so bad that she couldn't manage it. It didn't take her long to reach the youth, but when she arrived she found his limp body above water in Dega's arms. "Help me get him back," Dega said to her. "He's unconscious."

With the strength of both of them, the youth was pulled onto shore fairly quickly. He was a tall, lanky boy with curly brown hair and looked to be about sixteen years old. When he was lain down, Dega immediately began performing CPR, but it didn't seem to be working. The crowd that had gathered was still there, silent and breathless. Kandi couldn't bear the suspense. "Mr. Talladega?" she asked. He ignored her and kept trying to revive the boy. Almost a minute passed. "Let me," Kandi said, unwilling to feel so helpless.

"Are you certified?" he asked her quickly.

"No," she responded, "but I know how, and it doesn't seem like you're reviving him."

"I can't let someone who's not certified take my place." He paused momentarily and looked up. "Someone has called an ambulance, right?" No one responded and Dega's eyes widened. "*Call!*" he yelled. A woman standing near took out her cell phone and complied.

Another minute passed. The boy was still unconscious, and Dega—even as wet as he was from the water—was visibly sweating. He stepped away to rest for a few seconds, but as soon as he moved away, Kandi moved in. She pushed down in rhythm on the boy's chest, but her actions were as fruitless as Dega's. She took a huge breath directly above the boy's face and was about to move away when he suddenly opened his eyes and started coughing. A sigh escaped the lips of her watchers in unison, and they clapped before dispersing.

Dega came to the boy's side. "They've called an ambulance for you; you'll be okay."

"To be honest," he said, not at all breathless, "I don't think I'll be needin' one. I actually feel pretty good."

"Your lungs had to be filled with water," Dega told him curiously. "You really shouldn't be able to talk right now."

15

"All I know is that I feel perfectly normal," he said, cracking a smile. "Thank you for that." He stuck his hand out toward Dega.

"She's the one to be thanked," Dega said, motioning at Kandi and not noticing the invitation to shake hands.

"Well, then thank you," he said, nodding to Kandi. "Eric Molony."

Eric's accent amused Kandi somewhat. "Kandi Jenkins," she replied.

Eric stood, his rescuers following suit, and looked at Dega. "I know it sure looks weird, but there's nothin' wrong." Kandi noted that Eric's pronunciation of *wrong* would rhyme with *home*. She smiled.

Kandi looked at Dega and saw the look she had only seen when someone asked him a health question he didn't know the answer to. "Yeah, I know," he said to Eric, still thinking hard. A moment passed. "I need to talk to you guys later in private. And Dru. My name is Dega Talladega, by the way," Dega told him, realizing he hadn't yet done so.

Eric nodded in acknowledgment of Dega's name and then asked, "What are you wantin' to talk about?"

"You'll see when we meet. Can you guys come by my condo tonight around eight? I'll have a few pizzas."

"We can," Kandi told him.

"You're makin' me a little nervous, but I think I might can be there," Eric said. Dega had to keep his expression straight when he read Eric's mind and found that he would be bringing a gun. "Can I bring a friend of mine?"

Dega breathed. "How close are the two of you?"

"Very."

"Then he's welcome to come," Dega told him, inwardly lamenting the fact. He gave directions, told Eric he would apologize to the people who would come with the ambulance, and the three of them parted ways.

Dega had been home for only a few minutes when he heard a knock on the door. He opened it to see Eric and a very muscular, red-headed boy who was almost as tall as Eric. The latter held out his large hand. "Barrett Parker," he said.

"Dega Talladega," Dega said, surprised that a teen would have a grip as firm as Barrett's.

"Thank you for lettin' me come," he said to Dega kindly.

"Of course," Dega replied. He turned his attention to Eric. "Do you still feel okay?"

"Yeah," Eric replied, laughing. "I've been just fine."

Dega nodded. "Come on in and make yourselves at home. We'll eat as soon as Dru and Kandi get here."

They went into an open living and kitchen area. Since Dega was the only one living there, aside from a couch, a coffee table, and a television, the only accommodations were folding chairs. Eric and Barrett sat in the chairs. "Do you want us to pay some for the pizzas?" Barrett offered.

"No, that's okay," Dega declined. "I invited you here."

Kandi and Dru arrived a few minutes later, introductions were made, and they ate. Dega took note that Eric's pistol was in the back of his jeans, concealed by his T-shirt.

"I hate to be so quick jumpin' into this," Eric started as he was getting his pizza, "but why am I here?"

"I've been thinking about how to explain it to you," Dega told him. "There's nothing I can say to make you believe me right now, so I thought it would be better explained by somebody in the same boat as you." He turned to Dru. "Would you care to tell them about our powers?"

Dru stiffened at the phrase *our powers*. "Are you serious?" It was obvious she wanted no involvement in such a conversation.

"I am."

Dru took a deep breath and looked at Kandi for help. Together they explained all that Dega claimed had happened to him and what he supposedly discovered. They voiced their thoughts on how unlikely it seemed with every event, and Dega interjected whenever he felt they left out an important detail; he stated everything as fact.

Eric and Barrett were obviously uncomfortable with Dega before the tale was even finished and so said nothing. Dega didn't need to read their thoughts to know what they were thinking. "I have proof," he told them. Eric's head shifted ever so slightly, indicating interest. "Dru, make your fire."

Dru looked at Dega, again wanting to disregard his words, but then realized it made no difference and consented. The light bulbs in the room suddenly seemed dim compared to the intensity of the flame that engulfed Dru when she stood. A few seconds later it was gone. "That was supposed to be fire?" Barrett asked, trying to make his eyes readjust.

"It *was* fire," Dega told him simply.

Eric tried to focus his eyes on Dega. "Just to make this conversation a little longer, let's say we believe y'all. What about it?" he asked.

"The powers get stronger when they're near other powers. Today when Kandi revived you, I felt my power double in strength. Both of you have a power; I'm fairly certain yours is water, and," he said, turning to Kandi, "yours is air."

"This is ridiculous," Barrett said. Eric cracked a smile of agreement.

Dega looked straight at Eric. "If I couldn't read your mind, how would I know about the pistol you brought with you?" he asked. Kandi and Dru raised their eyebrows. Eric straightened, shocked, and reached for his back. "Whoa, there, there's no need to pull it," Dega said quickly. "I don't have one, and I don't mind that you do; I was just showing you that I know what you're thinking."

"Get out of my head," Eric told him strongly.

"I only checked your attitude when you got here; I've not read you since."

Eric brought his hand back to his lap, empty.

"Why do you have a gun?" Kandi asked worriedly.

Eric almost laughed. "I don't know y'all. And carrying guns is normal where we're from."

Dru looked at Barrett. "Do *you* have one?"

Barrett smiled. "Not on me. We figured if somethin' happened and somebody searched us, we'd better have another one hidden somewhere."

"Back to my point," Dega said, tiring of off-topic conversation, "I can read your mind. And you can manipulate water. Try to imagine water in some form in the middle of the room, and then make it."

"There's no way—" Eric started but stopped when he saw a big blue "T" before him; its appearance unnerved him so much that he almost let the water drop onto the floor.

"Be careful," Dru, the only one with experience enough to notice, told him.

Dega opened a window. "Kandi, make a soft breeze," he said. Kandi was in so much shock that what he said didn't even register for a moment. "Are you trying?" he asked.

Kandi concentrated and eventually everyone in the room felt a very light movement of air particles. "Good," Dega said, "now push Eric's T out the window."

19

It was gradual at first, but soon the entire T, formless now, was outside. Eric and Kandi let it drop.

"Do you guys believe me now that we are the Destined of old?" Dega asked.

"Yes," Dru told him.

"Me too," Kandi put in.

Eric hesitated. "Give me time to think about it. You've gotta remember, this is the first I'm hearin' of it."

Dega nodded and looked at Barrett, who quickly said, "Y'all could seriously just be messin' with me right now, so I'm gonna go with *no*."

"Even after seeing what Eric did?" Dega asked, surprised.

Barrett smiled nervously. "Technology's pretty good nowadays."

"Ah," Dega said.

"So," Eric started, "what is it that you're tellin' us is our *mission*, or whatever you're sayin' it is?"

"We don't know," Dega responded. "We have to wait for the other two powers to show themselves."

Barrett's face showed amusement. "Makes sense," he said, laughing.

"Well, I've said my peace," Dega said. "You guys are welcome to stay and talk about it or change the subject, but I'm done."

"In that case, we'd better be gettin' back to the hotel," Barret said. "Thank you for the pizza, Mr. Talladega."

During their time in Miami, Kandi experimented with air. For the biggest experiment she had performed in the ocean, she did the following: as a wave approached her, she imagined the wind blowing against it and changing its direction. She almost fell over when she realized that she had actually caused that to happen for a small width of the wave—convincing her that she could indeed control it as Dru could control fire. Dru was happy for Kandi, and Kandi was absolutely giddy for them both. On the trip home, Dru reminded Kandi that there was supposedly going to be some kind of horrible thing they would have to confront, to which Kandi replied that the United States military was the best that had ever existed, and the "Destined" might not even have any work to do.

A few days after arriving home, Kandi answered the door to see Dru, looking even more sullen than normal. "What's wrong?"

Dru spoke softly. "We're moving."

Kandi's eyes widened. "You're *moving*?" she asked, astonished.

"Yeah. My parents both got jobs with some lodging company in Tennessee."

Kandi was still dumbfounded. "You can't convince them to stay here?"

"You know how they are," Dru answered, taking a breath. "There's nothing I can do."

"Maybe you could stay with us ..."

Dru shook her head. "It would be bad for their image to adopt a kid and then leave her with other people." She paused again. "I'm going to be surrounded by a bunch of rednecks."

Kandi laughed at Dru's outlook. "Eric and Barrett weren't that bad, remember?"

"True." Dru sighed. "We're leaving tomorrow."

Kandi's mouth dropped. "That soon?" she asked. Dru nodded. "Wow. Can you stay here a little while?"

"Yeah, I guess," said Dru. "I need to get home and pick out everything that doesn't go in the boxes that the movers are going to take, though."

For the next few hours they lay on Kandi's bed, just talking. The conversation eventually moved to Kandi's family and to her brother Bradley. "Where's he stationed now?" Dru asked.

"I'm not sure," Kandi told her. "Somewhere in East Tennessee."

Dru sat up. "Idea!"

"What?" Kandi sat up and looked at Dru strangely.

"Could we talk your mom into letting you come stay with us for a little while if we promised to go see him?"

Dru could see Kandi's mind working through what she had just said.

Kandi smiled.

Dega answered his door. "Hey, what's up?" he asked Dru and Kandi.

"We're both moving to Gatlinburg, Tennessee," Kandi said hesitantly, curious what his response would be.

Dega's face brightened. "That's great!"

"How so?" Dru asked.

"That moves the Destined closer together," he told her. "How did that happen?"

"My parents got a job with a lodging company," Dru began, "and we were going to ask Kandi's parents if she could come stay with us for a while, but when we brought it up, they realized they wanted to be closer to her brother, who's stationed near there, and they made a few calls, found jobs, and decided they would come, too."

"Fate is an amazing thing," Dega told her.

"But away from the only one who has any idea what's going on," Kandi noted.

Dega closed his eyes and concentrated, and—even though they didn't know what he was doing—Dru and Kandi had enough sense to not say anything until he was finished. After a few awkward moments he opened his eyes. "There just happens to be an opening at a school near Gatlinburg; I think I can help them out a little."

Eric and Barrett walked up and down the aisles at the local grocery store. "What else?" Eric asked, referencing the list Barrett's mom had given him.

"Just bread and we're good," Barrett responded.

They started for the bread aisle, but Barrett stopped before they reached it. "Is that ...?"

Eric followed Barrett's eyes. "Yeah, I think it is," he said, laughing. "That's odd."

The two of them walked over to the girls they had recognized. "Y'all aren't from around here, are ye?" Barrett asked.

Kandi and Dru turned toward the voice. "Hey!" Kandi greeted. "What are you guys doing?"

Barrett laughed. "Shoppin'," he told them. "What are y'all doin' down here?"

"My parents got jobs here," Dru answered, "and hers wanted to be closer to her brother. He's in the military, stationed near here."

Eric looked at Barrett, and Barrett knew he was thinking it all was related to what Dega had told them in Miami about powers. "Is Mr. Talladega coming?" Barrett asked.

"Yeah, he'll be here in a few days," Kandi told him.

"What are your parents gonna be doin' down here?" Eric asked Dru.

"They were hired by a lodging company."

Eric tilted his head. "My parents own a lodging company ... my last name's Molony."

"That's who hired them," Dru said, a little surprised.

Barrett looked down at his phone. "Mom just texted me. They're wantin' us back pretty soon."

"Your mom *texts*?" Eric asked, feigning amazement.

Barrett laughed and looked up at Kandi and Dru. "Y'all are more than welcome to come out to the farm sometime if you want. Mom's a really good cook."

Dru and Kandi said that they might take him up on his offer, and the two groups parted ways.

Barrett's snoring kept his dog, Scout, wide awake the entire night. The side of his face was planted on his desk and his "pilot hat" was tilted on his head, close to sliding off. It was the night after they had seen the girls from their vacation, and he didn't think he would ever forget how strange everything turned out to be.

When he had returned home from his vacation, he still had mixed feelings about Eric, and he contemplated on whether or not he would believe them. He had never been so pensive or envious in his whole life. Yes, he was very envious of his best friend. Barrett wanted a power. He wanted that sort of responsibility, if their powers really existed.

He had stayed up until about three o'clock in the morning laying in his bed, pondering everything about "The Destined" and their so-called *powers* or *gifts*, things that a normal person wouldn't believe. And finally, his emotions—the things he wondered about, the possibilities—got to him. He had turned on his desk lamp and computer and searched the Internet for whatever might help him with this situation. He wanted to find out more about "The Destined"—if there was such a thing. He scanned the same exact web pages as Dega Talladega once had years before, but Barrett took everything differently. In fact, he didn't *take* anything.

Barrett was not convinced. The information on the Internet was not enough to make him believe in the legend. But he tried to comprehend it, and in his attempt, he set his elbows on his desk and drove his thumbs into his temples and winced. Then, he extended his arm toward the wall behind the desk—letting the arm rest on the desktop—and placed the side of his head on his arm. He fell fast asleep.

"Bear, your dad needs help in the field!" Janie Parker yelled, as she had been for her son for almost five minutes, "You'd better hurry ... I think there's a storm comin'!"

Barrett raced out of his room, through the hall, through the kitchen, and out the door of the house. He ran toward the field where his dad was tending to their nearly four hundred cows. The Parkers had lived on a three-hundred-ninety-acre farm for as long as he could remember—all sixteen years of his life. He understood how farm life was. He knew it meant business when his dad needed his help. His dad, Kenneth Parker, hardly ever asked for assistance; he was a strong man and could do most of the chores by himself. He was known for being the best diesel mechanic in all of Sevier County; that's where he got his money. Every trucker who came through the county would ask for *Pete Parker*—that's what everyone called him—before they made it completely through. He was like a celebrity, and Barrett was very proud to be his son.

Barrett finally reached his dad, who was heaving hay bales onto a platform for the cattle to eat. Kenneth's long, blonde hair was swaying, for there were strong winds brewing, and the sky was starting to turn a stormy shade of grey.

"Hurry, Bear, the storm's comin' fast!" Kenneth yelled as he heaved a hay bale on the platform.

The air got crisp and made Barrett shiver as he ran to the trailer, which had four hay bales left. He couldn't lift them as well as his father, but nonetheless, he lifted a bale, set it on the platform, and pushed it forward. In the time that it took him to lift only the one bale, his dad had lifted two and set them on the platform.

Barrett then rushed to finish unloading the last bale of hay, for the storm was brewing low in the sky over Barrett's head. He felt a drop of water hit his shoulder. Yeah, it was rain. More and more raindrops started to fall around where he and his dad were. Barrett turned to look at his dad, who had just finished unloading the last bale.

Looking up at the storm and its enormous grey beauty, he heard his father grunt behind him to let him know it was time to run back to the house. Barrett started through the field. It had high grass that would only get higher after such a massive storm. It looked like it would be the worst storm to ever hit Gatlinburg. And, with this scary thought, Barrett started to run faster.

The rain began to pour harder. Barrett's clothes were quickly soaked through; the legs of his jeans were already drenched because of the wet, high grass he had been sprinting through. There was lighting all around, and it seemed as if it was closing in on Barrett and his dad. The thunder was so loud that Barrett couldn't hear himself think. He started sprinting faster and faster, trying get across the huge field as quickly as possible.

Suddenly, Kenneth saw a flash of light come down from the vast clouds above. The light blinded him, and the force of shock caused him to stop in his tracks and fall to the ground unconscious.

When Kenneth gained consciousness and opened his eyes, he heard the screams and shrieks of what sounded like his son. Kenneth realized it *was* Barrett.

The pain was too much for Barrett; he was screaming in a way that he had never done before. He had never been in this much pain. He had been struck by lightning, and now he was on the ground, soaking wet and screaming in the most horrid tone his father had ever heard. His tears were drenching his face, while his clothes were soaked with rainwater.

Kenneth raced up to his son, who seemed as if he were being gruesomely tortured, as if he were in some sort of eternal electric chair. He burst into tears when he saw his son in this sort of excruciating pain. He didn't know what to do. He was in the middle of a nightmare. His son could be dying right before his eyes and he couldn't even help. The tears and sorrow threw him to his knees. Kenneth looked up to the dark grey vastness and watched the rain fall through the sky around him and onto his already drenched face.

Barrett had stopped screaming and lay so still that he seemed to be dead, which was what Kenneth thought. He was convinced that his son was now dead because of a catastrophe he was unable to stop or control. He had to try to wake him since there was nothing else he could possibly do. He pushed his son, but it was like pushing on a rag doll.

"Bear! Wake up!" Kenneth shouted, "Come on, Son! Wake up!"

Kenneth's tears were streaming down his face. He was on his knees in the middle of a field, soaking wet with rainwater and his son, who seemed to be dead—he *had* to be dead—laying before him. Kenneth lost all sympathy for everything around him. The storm, the rain, the wind, the tears, the lightning that was still above him in the clouds; they all meant nothing to him at this moment. He had lost all senses and ability to care for things, other than the fact that his one and only son might have died right before his eyes.

Barrett flinched. His body started to shiver, and he was making sudden movements like he was having a seizure. His eyes were blinking rapidly and his pupils were dilating. His head started shaking and moving; his whole body was contorting. Kenneth's first thought was, *he's alive!* But then it slowly changed to: *What's happening? Is that a seizure?*

Suddenly, Barrett stopped shaking and took in a long gasp of air. His eyes opened wide, but they didn't move at all. Then he started coughing, trying to get air and gain full consciousness. He leaned up and looked at his dad, who was now crying tears of joy, for his son wasn't dead after all.

"Dad ... what happened?"

"I honestly don't know, Son. Are you okay, though? Can you walk? We need to get back in the house and out of these wet clothes."

Barrett stood up like nothing had happened. He seemed fine. It was amazing; Kenneth couldn't believe it. He was still crying tears of happiness to add to the rain still pouring on him and his son. They finally made it to the house.

"Son, don't you dare tell your mother what just happened. You look just fine, and she doesn't need anything to worry about. So this will just be our secret. All right?"

"All right, Dad."

"Y'all are all soaked!" Janie called out from the kitchen. "What's the matter with you, Ken, stayin' outside so long?"

Barrett smiled, left his dad to explain however he chose, and walked upstairs. He quickly dried off and changed clothes before calling Eric to let him know what had just happened— not so much that he had been struck by lightning, but that he, Barrett, had the power of lightning.

CHAPTER 3

"So what now?" Barrett asked, his annoyance beginning to show. He, Dega, Eric, Kandi, and Dru had gathered in the cabin Dega was renting from Eric's dad. Dega had decorated the cabin in about the same way as he had his beach house but with more rustic furniture.

"I don't feel like there's anything we can do," Dega told him calmly.

Barrett was unhappy with Dega's answer. "So we're just gonna sit here and do nothin', even though we have five people with powers? That's really what you're thinkin' is the best idea, Mr. Talladega?"

"We're not really doin' *nothin',*" Eric said calculatingly. "We're waitin' for the sixth power."

"'Wait," Barrett said, using Eric's word. "We've been waitin' for almost a year. We need to *do* somethin'. Doesn't it make havin' the powers pointless if all we do is sit around?"

"A lot of times, waiting is best," Dega told him softly. "Think about it this way: What is there to do right now?" Barrett was silent, thinking. "You can't think of anything. That's because there *isn't* anything."

"There's gotta be somethin'," Barrett protested. "I have trouble believin' that keepin' this bottled up really is the best solution here."

"*Bottled up*," Dega said aloud. "We probably should tell your parents."

Dru laughed. "You think they'll still let us even *talk* to you if we bring this up to them?"

Dega cocked his head. "If we do it right."

"Well," Eric started, "might as well go ahead an' call 'em."

They called and, surprisingly, all their parents were free. They told their parents only that there was something that concerned all of them and that they needed to talk.

Sean and Brenna Molony arrived first—the former looked at his son quizzically as he entered— and not long after they were followed by Janie and Kenneth. Travis and Emmalynn Jenkins and Vinson and Vera Drake pulled into the driveway at the same time, about fifteen minutes later.

When the chatter ceased, Dega stayed quiet for a moment before he spoke. "This is going to be a little strange for you guys to hear," he said, "but listen before you reject it. I wish I could get them to explain it." He motioned toward the teenagers in the room and added, "but I think it will come better from me." He then told the tale of his findings in college for the umpteenth time. The story ended only after every detail had been mentioned, right up through Barrett's lightning.

"We don't mess with believin' stuff like that down here," Sean said when he was finished. "You know me and your mom better than that, Eric."

"Wait a second, Sean," Kenneth said to him, trying to convey his sense of cautiousness. He looked at Janie. "I didn't figure it'd have helped anything to worry you, but that part about Barrett gettin' struck by lightnin' is true." Janie almost jumped out of her seat. "He's fine; he's fine," Kenneth said, trying to calm her. "It took a minute, but he hopped up like it was nothin', and to this day I still have no idea how that's possible." He turned to Dega. "I don't believe you, but I know that somethin' odd's goin' on."

"The strangest part is that we're still here," Vera put in, shaking her head. "I have better things to do than listen to this nonsense. You should be ashamed of yourself." She looked at Dega and stood to leave.

"We have proof," Kandi told her carefully.

"If," Eric said, "y'all would be willin' to stay an' see it."

"I like the sound of seein' somethin'," Kenneth said, trying to convince Vera to sit.

Vinson laughed. "I didn't have anything planned for today, did you?"

Vera sat.

"That was as well received as I expected, I guess," Dega voiced. "We're asking you to trust us, but we're not asking blindly. Eric, could you start?"

"Yeah," Eric agreed.

Brenna saw her son's eyes focus sharper than any eyes she had seen before, and soon she noticed that her shirt was getting damp. She looked around and saw that everyone else was having the same problem. If she squinted, she could see tiny water droplets moving—seemingly—from Eric to them.

"How are you making my shirt wet?" Travis asked.

Eric smiled and sat back down.

"Kandi?" Dega asked.

She stood up, and her body stilled. Brenna noticed that, instead of focusing, her stare went completely blank, almost hazed. Then Kandi breathed out a long breath, and a breeze could be felt throughout the room, eventually drying the shirts dampened by Eric. This time no one spoke; they waited silently for the next demonstration.

"Dru."

Dru stood and, arms down at her side, made her palms face forward. They glowed slightly, but they brightened quickly and a flame engulfed her body. She took a few steps toward the parents—who could hardly bear to look at her—allowing them to feel the heat before she allowed the fire to dissipate as she sat down.

Dega looked at Barrett, who waited until everyone had finished rubbing their eyes before he began. "I'm gonna send a shock through y'all," he told the parents, who, conveniently, were seated in what was nearly a smooth curve. He touched Vinson, who was sitting on the end, and watched everyone's reactions as the shock traveled from person to person. When it reached Brenna, who was seated on the other end, it visibly flew through the air back to Barrett.

Dega stood and walked to Travis and Emmalynn, whom he knew to be the most reluctant to believe. "Would one of you hold out your arm?" Out of curiosity, Emmalynn did as instructed, and Dega noticed a thin line of discoloration near her wrist. He let his hand hover over it for a few seconds and sat back down.

Emmalynn looked at her arm in amazement. "What did you do ... ?"

Dega was going to let the action speak for itself, but when Janie called it a miracle, he responded by saying that only the Creator could perform miracles; the healing power possessed by Dega was limited.

None of the parents fully believed, but nor did any fully disbelieve. It was obvious there was *something* to what they had been told, and each independently decided to go along with whatever they were told, just in case their children were right.

A black sports car, followed by a red pickup truck, pulled into a small parking lot. In the middle of the lot was an edifice resembling a cabin, but it was actually a restaurant. The roof was a blue metal; it was a stereotypical Southern restaurant. The sign in the middle of the parking lot had *Blue Ridge Restaurant* written on it in blue letters.

Eric, Barrett, and Dega stepped down from the truck, and Kandi and Dru exited the sports car; together, the five of them walked up the porch steps and into the restaurant. The inside looked as Kandi had predicted: homey and quaint; the smell of food enveloped her immediately. She and her friends sat down and enjoyed the conversation and fellowship.

There weren't very many people in the restaurant, but one man stood out to them. In fact, he stood out to everyone when he called out loudly, "Y'all look!" Of course, everyone looked at the television screen to which he was pointing; the news was on.

> "Breaking News: Military bases and large cities all over the world are being attacked. The US missile defense system seems to have been hit, and we're told that the majority of the debris is on course to hit right in the heart of Glasgow. The US government hasn't responded, as the missiles that hit New York and Washington were undetected, and it's unclear which country is responsible. As far as our intelligence can tell, every nation has been hit to about the same extent. Stay with us as ..."

The restaurant was silent; the customers and servers were in shock—not moving, barely breathing. The only things they were able to process mentally were fear and prayer. Eventually everyone left, presumably to check on their families, and the five friends were the only souls remaining in the building.

Kandi opened her mouth, but her first attempt at speaking ended in the release of a single breath. "How could ...?" she finally managed.

"Evil is strong," Dega said, his voice understandably monotone. "They want money and power, I assume. But I can't understand how they could be willing to kill so many people to get it, either."

Barrett found words to speak. "If every country's been hit equally, this could already be the deadliest war in history," he said.

"The deadliest war in history ..." Eric repeated. "Y'all don't think ...?"

"That this is what we're destined to do?" Dega said, finishing Eric's thought.

"If it's not," Barrett started, "I'd sure hate to see what it actually ends up bein'."

"We can't just walk up to people with that many weapons and try to fight," said Dru, who, for the first time in her life, was trying unsuccessfully to hold back tears.

"No, we can't," Dega agreed. "We'd need a well-thought-out plan."

"Cell phones aren't working," Kandi said, looking up.

Eric checked his. "In that case, we'd better be gettin' home."

"You should," Dega agreed, "but one thing before we go: stay here in Gatlinburg. Even if your parents want to leave, tell them you can't. We need to stay here. Plus, out here in the middle of nowhere—no offense—" he looked at Eric and Barrett, "it's not very likely we'll be attacked."

They agreed, still a little shaken up, and went home. Their

parents had indeed been worried and were busy trying to contact relatives in other areas of the country.

Dega turned everything on at home when Eric dropped him off: the radio, the television, the computer; he knew they needed to know as much about the attacks as possible if they were going to try to fight. It was immediately apparent that the news stations were blaming Iran for the attack, but Dega knew Iran wasn't behind them; he didn't know why he knew, but he did.

After listening to the coverage of the attacks for only a few minutes, it was obvious that they needed to act, and it couldn't wait. At first, he wanted to give his friends at least another night at home, but as more and more attacks were reported, he realized they couldn't even wait that long. The land lines were still operational—in Gatlinburg, at least—and he called everyone and told them they needed to be at his cabin in two hours. They—and their parents, for that matter—would have to understand.

Dru had no problem with leaving; she looked at it as an escape from her adoptive parents. Kandi, on the other hand, almost couldn't do it. She was very attached to both her parents and thought it a miracle that she had the emotional strength to leave them. Eric and Barrett both tried to use reason to cloud their emotions and so were able to leave with minimal tears. None of the parents liked the idea very much, but they saw no way of physically stopping their children and so consented.

They all arrived on Dega's porch at the time specified with bags, anxiety, and tears. Thirty minutes later they departed together, knowing nothing except what they had decided would be their priority: save the United States of America.

CHAPTER 4

Barrett woke early, as usual, to the sounds of the forest coming alive—the birds singing, the squirrels playing, and the wind whistling through the trees just a few yards away. He got out of bed, dressed, and walked outside. The sun was just coming up, which made for a spectacular scene. He walked around for about half an hour, getting his bearings in his new environment. The trees were very dense throughout almost the whole wood, and Kandi had covered their tracks well; no one would find them or even think to look at a cabin owned by Eric's family. They would never have to worry about food either, because the creek was filled with fish. He decided that gathering firewood was the least he could do to be productive. It wasn't cold—the Georgia summers didn't allow for that even at night—but the fire Dru would make to cook the fish would have to sustain itself. He quickly retrieved more than an acceptable amount of kindling and, not wanting to return so soon from the peacefulness to Eric's family's cabin, sat down on the soft ground to relax.

Soon he found himself thinking back on the previous day's events. When they left Dega's cabin, there had been arguing about what to do, but eventually they decided that—since a vote would have ended in a five-way tie—listening to Dega was the sensible thing to do. He suggested they go somewhere they couldn't be found and where they wouldn't be attacked, so they could think through what exactly was to be done. Now here they were, Barrett walking around in the woods and everyone else sleeping. He would have been more than content to stay by himself for hours, but he decided it had been long enough and he needed to get back.

As he neared the cabin, he began to hear the distinct off-pitch of Eric's whistling to himself. "Mornin'," Barrett greeted him when he entered the clearing.

Eric stopped whistling and turned. "Hey," he responded from the porch.

Barrett put the wood next to the fire pit. "Anybody else up?" Eric asked. He laughed, and Barrett smiled. "Didn't figure so but thought I'd ask."

"We might be havin' to go get 'em if they sleep much longer," Eric told him. "I'm gettin' anxious."

"Seriously," Barrett said, sitting down in the chair beside him. "Is there anything to eat inside?"

Eric shook his head. "Trust me, I checked. Nana cleaned out when they left the last time they were out here."

"Sounds about right," Barrett agreed. They were quiet a moment. "Wanna go get some fish?"

Eric stood. "Yeah, that sounds pretty good."

The two of them walked around to the back of the cabin to get a bag. "I'm assumin' we won't need a fishin' pole?" Barrett asked.

"Shouldn't," Eric replied, grinning.

They left the cabin and walked to the creek. Eric didn't hesitate; he immediately went to the bank and concentrated, and soon Barrett saw the water directly in front of Eric quickly fade into the other side of the stream. The water that should have flowed into what was now a dry bed was diverted by a current, and Barrett was able to walk out and put ten fish in the bag; there were more, but they needed only the ten. He got out of the creek bed and Eric, with a big smile on his face, released the current to flow as it would.

"That's the kind of thing that does away with doubt," he said to Barrett.

"It really is," Barrett agreed.

They walked back to the clearing and set the fish down by the fire pit. "You know what I just realized?" Eric asked. "We were both probably thinkin' Dru, but *you* could actually start the fire."

Barrett realized how obvious it was and was amused that he hadn't thought of it. He put the firewood in the pit, told Eric to move back, and hoped his lightning bolt wouldn't be too strong. From his hand came a very small one, and a flame started perfectly. Eric put the fish above it to cook.

They stayed outside talking until the fish were almost done, and then Eric went inside and woke Dega. "Mornin'. Breakfast is ready outside."

Dega sighed groggily. "Okay, I'll be out there in a minute."

Eric knocked on the girls' door and, with some loud noises, woke them up and told them the same.

Barrett served fish on paper plates that Eric's grandparents kept in the cabin, and they sat down to eat on the porch. "Any suggestions?" Dega asked. He didn't have to mention the topic.

"Kill the terrorists without gettin' ourselves killed is one plan," Eric said.

Kandi nodded and laughed. "I like it."

Dega shook his head and smiled. "*How*, though?" he asked.

"We need to know what's goin' on," Barrett said seriously. "Somehow we've gotta stay connected to everybody else, like with TV or somethin'."

"That's going to be hard to do," Dru put in. "There probably is too much destruction for the news channels to keep up. Or even to stay running."

"Okay," Dega said, "so we're narrowing down our goals. Now: *how?*"

"Who would know the most about what's happening?" Kandi asked. "We could get close to them."

Eric thought a moment. "The military, I'd guess."

Dega's eyes lit up. "And we already have a connection."

"Who's that?" Barrett asked.

"Kandi's brother, Bradley."

"Oh, that's right," Eric said. "I'd forgotten about that."

"So we go talk to Bradley," Dru said with a hint of finality in her voice. "What do we tell him?"

"The truth," Kandi replied simply.

"You think he's not gonna go tell his superiors we're crazy or anything?" Eric asked.

"He won't," Kandi told him confidently. "He has an open mind and does what's right even if he has to disobey orders to do it."

"Me an' him are gonna get along," Barrett said, laughing. "When should we leave?"

"Now," Dega told him. "Wasting time will do us no good." He turned to Kandi. "Where's he stationed again?"

"On one of the mountains in Cherokee National Park."

"Who are y'all?" a voice said as they approached the entrance to the base. They had had to leave the van at the bottom of the mountain and had come two miles up on foot; in a way this was better, since they had a chance to learn the surrounding landscape. It had been obvious when they neared the base; the trees began to appear in rows rather than being randomly spaced.

Dega was about try to talk their way in, but Kandi spoke before he got the chance. "We're here to see my brother, Bradley Jenkins."

The guard pulled out his radio and requested that Bradley come meet them.

"Is it really that easy?" Eric asked, surprised.

The guard put his radio back in his pocket. "Not usually, but with all these attacks and people running in and out, checking on their families, deserting, prepping, and whatever else they're doing, protocol is pretty much done."

Dru wasn't satisfied. "I thought that the military trained to be ready for bad things like this."

"For bad things, yes," the guard responded, "but not for this."

Dega was not thrilled that the terrorist attacks had been bad enough to limit the following of base security of the United States Military, but he kept it to himself and watched a young man resembling Kandi appear from around the side of a building.

"Bradley!" Kandi screamed when she saw him. She ran toward him—Dru and Barrett looked at the guard to make sure he wouldn't try to stop her—and into his waiting arms.

"It's been way too long," Bradley told her, smiling. For the first time he noticed the rest of Kandi's group. "Hello," he said.

"Let's go to wherever you're staying and we can all talk," Kandi said, not wanting others to hear what they were about to tell him.

"Okay," he agreed, obviously curious about Kandi's unwillingness to explain immediately. He led them through the rows of identical buildings to the one in which he was quartered. Upon entering the barracks, he told them that all three of his roommates had left when the attacks began; two had gone to briefly check on family, but the third had simply vanished one day.

"That actually works out better," Kandi responded. She made introductions, and Dega explained to Bradley the basics of the powers, ending with quick demonstrations and the statement that this generation's Destined were supposed to stop the attacks.

"I don't necessarily believe that," Bradley said to Dega when he was done, "but if I did, what do you guys need?"

"We're needin' to know about everything that happens when it happens," Barrett answered him.

Bradley hesitated. "We don't have the kind of monitoring systems here that you would want; you'd have to be at a bigger base for that. Do you need to stay here?"

"We can go wherever we can get the most work done," Dega told him.

"I'm being transferred to Washington the day after tomorrow." Bradley scrunched his eyebrows in thought. "They still run a tight ship up there, but I might be able to get you in."

Eric nodded. "We'll take whatever help we can get."

"Well, considering it's a base, this isn't *too* bad," said Kandi after they arrived in the two-bedroom, one-living room residence where they would be staying in Washington while Bradley was away following orders. After a half hour-long discussion—without mention of the powers—General Freed had finally agreed to let them stay on base, the only stipulation being that they go nowhere without being accompanied by a soldier, not even down the hall.

"This will—"

Dega cut Barrett off with a look that said *stop talking.*

"—be just fine," Barrett said, ending his sentence.

Dega grabbed a pen and paper and quickly wrote a note.

> *Be careful what you say. I read the general's mind; there's a bug in each room. Give me a second.*

Dega went into the room Eric and Barrett would be sharing and after a few minutes motioned everyone inside and closed the door. "I assumed disabling the bug in the guys' bedroom would be much less suspicious than either of the others. Don't mention anything about the powers in the other rooms."

Eric nodded. "So what now?"

"We just need to start gathering information," Kandi responded. "Mr. Talladega can read people's minds, and the rest of us can just keep our ears open."

Dega shook his head. "The people here know next to nothing. It doesn't seem like that will change."

For the next few days, they walked among large groups of soldiers as discreetly as possible when Bradley was with them, and when he wasn't, they sat in their living room watching the news while Dega searched minds. It quickly became apparent that Dega had been right; the only new thing they learned was the death toll: thirty million had died for sure, but the number could have been as high as one hundred million, depending on whom you believed.

"I'm getting anxious," Dru said one afternoon after a few hours of doing nothing.

"You'll need to learn to control that—" Eric remembered they were in the living room. "—soon."

Dru tried to think of a way to voice her response without giving anything away to anyone listening. "That's a lot easier for you, *water boy.*"

Eric laughed at the football reference but realized she had a point; water, by nature, was a calmer substance than fire.

"Y'all come here a minute," Barrett said calmly from his bedroom.

Kandi, Dru, and Eric entered to find Dega sitting still, eyes closed. Barrett shut the door, and Dega lifted his head to show a grim expression. "Somebody go let Bradley in. I'll tell you what's going on if he doesn't."

Kandi reached the door and opened it right before Bradley knocked. He looked at her strangely and followed her to Dega. Barrett shut the door again.

"The base is on lockdown, if they haven't told you," Bradley said simply.

"What?" Kandi asked, surprised.

"They detected missiles coming toward the base."

"*What?*" Dru said, more worried than Kandi.

"I know," Bradley said. "A little scary."

"But why'd we go on lockdown?" Eric asked. "Missiles sure aren't anything new, and they've not got anything to do with anybody that's actually on base."

Bradley seemed to be searching for something to say, so Dega, growing impatient, spoke up. "They were detected just in time to be blown up without causing too much damage. That shouldn't have happened, and the only possible reason is that someone messed with the base's detection equipment."

"I didn't say it," Bradley said, assuring himself of his innocence.

"Will they try to blame us?" Eric asked.

"They couldn't." Dega sounded certain. "There are cameras outside our doors and windows."

Dru hadn't yet gotten over her shock. "Next time, we might not catch them in time …" Her voice trailed off.

"Don't worry about it," Kandi told her, smiling. "If the equipment still managed to catch it this time, it will next time. If there even is a next time."

"That's right," Bradley echoed his sister. "I'm sorry to tell you this, but General Freed said that, since you *are* visitors, you're not allowed to leave here for any reason." He gave Kandi a hug and left.

When Barrett heard the door to the hallway shut, he turned to Dega. "Tell me if this makes sense: my power is lightnin', but with what modern science tells us, it could just as well be called *electricity*, right?"

"Yeah, I would agree with that." Dega said, not seeing his point.

"Would that make me good with electronics?"

"Yes," Dega replied, "with anything that requires electricity." Barrett got a sly smile on his face. "What are you thinking?"

Barrett took out his cell phone. "That doesn't work, does it?" Dru asked.

"Cell towers are down, but the next buildin' over has wireless Internet," Barrett explained. "Imagine what I could hack …"

Kandi's eyes focused. "Are you serious?"

"Yeah," Barrett told her. "Give me a few hours, and I'll tell you everything our *loving* government is keepin' from us about this."

CHAPTER 5

One Month Later

What are we actually trying to do?" Dru asked as she and her friends moved along the southwest Kentucky highway in the van they had acquired. Barrett's search through government files back in D.C. had come up empty, and they had been learning nothing new, so they left the base. During the few weeks following, they spent their time moving around the region, trying to learn something useful, but they accomplished nothing. The only thing they knew for certain was that, while the death toll's rising had slowed, it was definitely above one hundred million.

"Waiting," Dega, who was driving, told her in his calming voice. Had it not been for him, Dru, Kandi, Eric, and Barrett would have gone home to spend their last days with their families; Dega convinced them of the importance of staying together.

"Yeah, you've been saying that literally since we left Gatlinburg," Dru said, thoroughly displeased. "What exactly are we waiting *for*?"

"New information that can help us."

"Can we please talk about something else?" Barrett begged. "Every time we have this conversation I lose a little bit more hope."

Dru breathed and nodded. "What do you want to talk about?"

"How about *that*?" Kandi asked in a ghastly voice.

"That ain't good," Eric said, seeing what Kandi was staring at.

Dru looked out their side of the van and immediately wished she hadn't; she saw remnants of what residents used to call their home, a place where kids could still walk miles down the road without worry.

Almost everything was burned. She saw where some well-built walls had withstood a missile, but in the distance everything was gone.

Dega turned onto a smaller road and went toward the destruction; a sign far enough away from the impact to still be standing read *Welcome to Oswego*. Upon actually entering what must have been the city limits, the destruction became all the more evident. There were no trees or cars, and the road was essentially nonexistent. Everything seemed dead.

"What happened?" Dru asked slowly.

"What's it look like?" Dega replied, pulling the van to a halt.

Everyone got out and looked around. "I don't ..." Kandi started before her voice failed her.

"It seems different to actually see it instead of just hearin' about it," Barrett noted, his words full of sorrow.

"When do you think it was hit?" Eric asked.

"I would say just a few days ago," Dega concluded after looking around for a few seconds.

Dru and Kandi had already started walking away from the vehicle and farther into the destruction. There were no signs of life, and no other living creatures were out in the open. It was eerie, not seeing or hearing even the smallest bird; the air was very still.

They came upon the remains of some sort of house. The walls were mostly destroyed, but they could see where a table had been, where a television had rested. Kandi couldn't stand the sight of it and moved on; Dru followed.

They both jumped when they heard an extremely loud cough—though the volume probably just seemed loud from being in a worse-than-ghost town and not having heard any sound for a few minutes. It startled them almost as much when Barrett, Eric, and Dega sprinted past them toward the sound of the cough.

"Where are you?" Barrett asked as they and the girls reached the place where the sound had originated.

"Here," came a weak reply.

Everyone rounded a wall, seemingly left from a church, and saw two men with Bibles in their hands. "Welcome to our church here," said the man with the weak voice. "I'm Lowell Taylor, the minister here, and this is Robert Callaway."

Eric introduced his party—not mentioning the powers at all—before asking, "What are y'all still doin' here?"

"I needed some ...counseling," Robert responded with a hint of hesitation in his voice. "I'm sure you can understand."

"Would it not make more sense to do that in a city that still has a good water supply and electricity?" asked Dru.

"I think this," said the minister, holding up his Bible, "is more important than electricity. And we have bottled water and food in the cellar."

"Which is where you were when the missile hit," Dega noted aloud, "explaining why you're still alive."

Tears came to Robert's eyes, and Lowell, noticing, put a

hand on his shoulder and said, "She's better off there than we are here."

Barrett allowed a moment of silence to pass before asking how long ago the missile had hit.

"Two days ago," Lowell answered him. "Two days ago we experienced what the fires of hell must be. Shrieks of friends, burning heat, momentary unconsciousness. Opening the cellar door to this. It was awful."

Kandi's heart went out to them; theirs was the saddest story she'd heard since Dru's. "What did you do?" she asked.

"We cried," Robert told her. "Then we searched for survivors and cried some more. After a few hours I realized I needed help, so I asked him."

"So y'all have just been sittin' here for the past forty-eight hours?" Eric asked, amazed.

"For the most part. We both needed comfort."

"Are you the only ones left?" Dru queried bluntly.

"No," Lowell told her. "One, Jacob Young, was in jail for assault, and then there's his guard, Blake Reel. Jacob was trying to escape through a tunnel he found, and Blake was going after him. Jacob was deep down in the tunnel when we were hit, so he's fine, but Blake had just started down. He was unconscious for about ten hours, and he was gashed pretty good by shrapnel; he's got some pretty bad wounds. Jacob won't leave because this is his hometown, and Blake's hurt too bad to move. We'd still be there with him, but this morning I told him he wouldn't live but another few hours, and he asked to die alone."

"Where is he?" Dega asked, not trying to conceal the urgency in his voice.

"He asked to die alone," Lowell repeated firmly.

"Look at me," Dega said to him. "I can help."

"He's two houses that way," Robert revealed, sensing Dega's seriousness.

Dega ran and everyone else followed. He immediately noticed how close to death Blake truly was. "I want you to be calm," Dega told him. Blake looked questioningly at Dega.

Dega knelt down and put a hand on Blake's heart. It was very faint, but with Dega's concentration, his heartbeat gradually got faster and stronger. He then moved his hand over Blake's face, legs, and chest, healing his gaping wounds and fixing a broken rib. Upon finishing, he stood.

"What did you do?" Lowell asked Dega harshly.

"I healed him."

"Impossible."

Blake startled everyone but Dega when he spoke and said, "I don't know how, but he did, and I'm willing to accept it."

Lowell started to say something, but Blake's comment mixed with a look Eric gave him kept him quiet.

"Can you walk, Blake?" Robert asked in wonder.

Blake stood to test it. "Yeah, actually." He turned to Dega. "Who are you?"

Dega mimicked Eric's introductions before turning to Lowell. "Are you sure that you three and Jacob are the only ones alive?"

"To be honest, the search we made wasn't very thorough," Lowell admitted. "You can understand our inability to think perfectly straight ..." He finished speaking as if he, too, were wanting assurance that it was all okay.

With Barrett and Kandi following, Dega rushed outside, closed his eyes, and concentrated. After a few moments he opened them and ran toward the less-devastated part of the city. "They're in here," he said when they reached the remains of a building.

They stepped inside and Dega yelled out, "Ramona? Ruby? Are you two in here?"

No answer.

"Is there a basement?" Barrett asked as Dega started moving.

"That's where I'm going."

They walked through the wreckage to the back of the building where Dega uncovered a door in the floor. He opened it and led the way down.

When Kandi's eyes adjusted to the light, she saw two female bodies lying unconscious on the ground, debris scattered about them.

"Are they ...?" Kandi asked.

"There's no way they're still here," Barrett said, his voice sounding somewhat drained.

While Dega walked to the women, he assured Kandi and Barrett that he could sense their minds in the basement. He reached them and healed them, just as he had done with Blake.

They were both somewhat dazed, but one was alert enough to ask, "What happened?"

"Oswego was hit by a missile," Dega told her bluntly, "and the two of you were knocked unconscious somehow. We're here to try to help."

The five of them momentarily conversed, and it was discovered that—as Dega had known—their names were Ramona Harper and Ruby Reed. Ruby owned the restaurant located on the ground level above where they stood and had asked Ramona, who was retired from construction, to check a crack in the walls of the basement just before the missiles hit.

"So how did you find us?" Ramona, the one who had spoken first, asked.

"Just be glad we did," Dega said to her.

"I don't like games, especially not now." Ruby's voice had a hint of hostility.

Dega nodded his head. "I assure you, this isn't a game. Let's just go back to Lowell, Blake, and Robert."

He started walking without giving either one a chance to object again, and Barrett followed suit. Kandi looked at Ruby and said, "We'll do everything we possibly can to help you. I know it seems cliché to say, but it is going to be okay."

Lowell was the first to see the two women approaching. "Ramona! Ruby!" he called out. "You're both alive!"

"Yeah, so we've been told," Ramona responded, smiling.

The Oswegans began talking sadly about the loss of their neighbors and hometown. Dega allowed it for a few minutes but then asked, "Wasn't there another person you said was still alive? Jacob, right?"

"That lowlife prisoner?" Blake asked rhetorically. "He's out by what's left of his house."

"Blake," Lowell scolded gently, "now is the time for us to be gettin' along."

"*Us*, yes," Blake agreed, "but not with him."

Lowell shook his head and turned to Dega. "I'll show you where he is."

Everyone followed Lowell except Blake and Robert, who stayed to keep Blake company.

Kandi looked around and tried to note everything they passed, but it was actually hard to tell what anything had been. "Jacob?" Lowell called after they had gone five or six blocks. "Where are you at?"

"Over here, Lowell," came the reply.

Lowell started toward Jacob's voice. "What have you been up to?"

"Just rememberin'. And thinkin'."

"Care to meet some friends?"

Jacob appeared out of his house; they had moved away from the blast area. When he saw Ruby and Ramona, he exclaimed, "Hey! Y'all are okay!" Then he noticed the rest of the party. "Afternoon," he said, nodding. He looked at Lowell, awaiting an introduction.

Eric introduced everyone for what seemed like the hundredth time, and Jacob asked, "So what are y'all doin' here?"

"They're here to ..." started Lowell. He then turned to Dega. "That's a really good question."

"And I would like it answered," Ruby said, her voice lacking the hostility it had previously had.

Dega quickly read the minds of his four companions. He himself was of the opinion that they shouldn't reveal their identities for safety's sake. For their own reasons, Kandi and Eric agreed with him, but Barrett and Dru disagreed and saw no problem letting the facts be known. The vote split, Dega went with his instinct. "We can help you get your town at least recognizable again."

Jacob started laughing. "You think this can be repaired?"

Dega nodded. "This ...is the sort of thing we're good at. If all six of you help, we shouldn't have too much trouble."

"Six?" Jacob said to him. "Have you not told 'em Blake's as good as dead, Lowell?"

Lowell reasoned momentarily within himself how to respond. "He's better."

Jacob's eyebrows rose. "Ignorance lives ..."

"*Jacob*," Lowell said in a scolding voice. Both he and Dega sensed that they were going to have a problem.

"I got a right to my opinion," Jacob retorted, defending himself.

"That doesn't mean your opinion is okay."

Eric tried to calm the situation. "How 'bout let's go back to where him and Robert are, and we can figure out how this is gonna go from there," he suggested.

No one felt the need to dispute.

As soon as Robert and Blake were within hearing distance, Dega said, "We've all had a long day, and I think we need to find a place to sleep before somebody says something they'll regret."

Lowell was in full agreement. "There's a big building still standing back the way you came in. That's—that *was*—a hotel. Y'all five can stay there."

"I feel so sorry for them," Kandi said to her four friends in the hallway of the one-story motel.

Dega nodded. "That's why I told them we'd help them out some."

Dru hadn't liked the idea. "And how do you expect us to get anything up? Have you seen this place? It could take literally years!"

"We can help restore some of the buildings in this part of the town during the day, and at night we can get the power lines and water pipes working."

"What is that, like, twenty hours a day?" Dru asked, exhausted at the very thought.

"It won't take more than a couple days, Dru," Barrett told her, though with his background, twenty hours every now and then was a normal occurrence.

"Well, since we'll need to be starting tomorrow, how about we all go ahead and go to bed?" Kandi asked; being around the Southerners was slowly changing her lexical approach.

"Sounds good," Dega said, "but first let me ask this: do we tell them who we are?"

Eric spoke up quickly. "There's no sense in havin' people askin' unnecessary questions that aren't helpin' anything."

"Unnecessary questions?" Barrett asked, sounding amused. "If we tell them who we are, I'd think they'd be more liable to help." It was obvious these two had their opinions set in stone.

"I'm with Barrett," Dru put in. "If we never tell anybody, we won't ever get very much information, so we might as well start being open now."

"Compromise ..." Kandi said, wanting to get rid of anything with even the slightest semblance of argument. "Let's just tell them that we're the only people working against the terrorists who have even a little hope of success."

"And why is that?" Dru asked, playing devil's advocate.

"Because we've got somethin' nobody else does," Eric said, backing Kandi up. "And y'all don't need to know more than that."

Barrett and Dru were momentarily silent, so Dega seized the opportunity. "That works."

"Good," Kandi said.

"Okay, I guess," Barrett said, sighing. "'Night y'all."

The next morning, all eleven congregated in the church building, and some of the bacon and biscuits from the cellar were cooked over a fire and eaten. "So are you really planning on helping us rebuild?" Ramona asked, taking a bite of bacon.

"That's what we told you," Dega replied, laughing. "We don't lie."

"Since y'all think it can be done," Robert started, "I'm looking to y'all for leadership." The other five agreed immediately. "What's first?"

Dega cleared his throat. "Before we can do much else, we need to rebuild standing structures. But obviously we're not going to be able to rebuild everything, and we'll only be able to use some brick—it will mostly have to be wood."

"I vote we rebuild the church building first," Lowell requested and, because no one would dare deny such a request, that's what they started on.

When the day was almost over, they were halfway through with the construction of the auditorium; Lowell had agreed to let that be the only part they rebuilt. The speed came from the use of the powers when the Oswegans were otherwise occupied and from Ramona's expertise.

"Well, I gotta admit," Jacob said, setting down his tools, "I was wrong and we're actually gettin' this done."

"Yeah, and it looks like it's almost time for bed," said Dega, anxious to get Eric and Barrett started on the part of the reconstruction that would be most worthwhile. "We'll see you guys in the morning."

He and his four companions walked to the motel. Dega suggested they wait about two hours before beginning to ensure that everyone else was at least down for the night. When the time had elapsed, Dega went outside and searched minds to see who was still awake and, as a pleasant surprise, found none.

"What are you guys going to need from us?" Dega asked Eric and Barrett as he walked back inside.

"They're all asleep?" Eric asked. Dega nodded.

"How much are we actually doin'?" Barrett questioned.

"Just enough so that the buildings they stay in have water and power," Dega answered him.

"I'd need electricity to get the pipes back workin'," Eric noted.

"I gotcha covered," Barrett responded. "What I'll need is metal poles or more wires that we can connect to the wires that haven't been obliterated."

Eric thought about how much time it would take to come up with the materials and said that he wouldn't need any help to start with. After more discussion, they separated; while everyone else went to look for metal, Eric traced where the pipes were underground by sensing where water had been recently. When he found where they had become dislodged, he pulled a stream of water from the river—which was almost eight miles away—through the ground, into the pipes, through the filtration system, and to the buildings they were to work on. He decided that he would just have to keep the stream going until they could insert the necessary pipes.

Meanwhile, the other party found where the electrical lines suddenly stopped; unlike the water pipes, which led away from the destruction, this led toward it.

"What first?" asked Kandi, ready to start.

"Mr. Talladega," Barrett began, "can you read minds of the people while they're sleepin'?"

"I can," Dega responded. "What do you need?"

"See if any of 'em know how far away the substation is."

Dega was silent for a few moments before getting a look of annoyance on his face. "Not a single one of them," he said, looking up.

"Then could you search the minds of anyone within twenty miles of here?"

Again, Dega paused for a few seconds, but this time when he looked up he said, "It's over five miles away."

Kandi cocked her head. "Would it not make more sense to just see where the closest line that still has electricity is?"

Barrett considered her comment before agreeing and commending her.

"We'll have to find that by walking," Dega pointed out, "but I doubt it's any more than a mile or two away."

Barrett concentrated and created a current of electricity running through the lines that were still there. He told them what he did and said, "That'll have to do until we actually go and find the end of the circuit. Where can we get some copper?"

"I can go back to the city we passed about an hour before we got here and get some," Dru offered. "How much do we need?"

"Only a little every five hundred feet," Barrett answered.

"By *a little* you mean ...?"

"About an inch."

Dru's eyebrows rose. "You expect to get power back to this town with five-hundred-foot gaps?"

"I can make the current jump that far, and once it's there it'll last until the power cuts out again."

"That's not possible," Dru disagreed.

"Trust me," Barrett said, "I can do it. I just need an inch for every five hundred feet." He finished his sentence with his voice weakening.

"Get about five feet of copper," Kandi said, offering her computations. "That's a few inches over." She noticed the strange look Dru was giving her. "What?" she asked.

"I'm tired," Barrett said, changing the subject.

"Yeah," Dru said laughing, "let's go to bed."

"No," Barrett said. "I mean, I feel ... drained."

"So do—" Dru cut her sentence off when she saw Barrett collapse.

Dega quickly knelt and read his mind. "Let go of the electric current you have flowing," he told him.

A few seconds later, Barrett's eyes opened and he sat up. "What was that?" he asked, cringing.

"You used too much power and got too weak," Dega told him matter-of-factly.

"What now?" Kandi asked.

"Sustaining something drains your power, which drains *you*."

"So none of us can do anything very long," Barrett said as he stood.

Dega shrugged. "You just have to practice. In a few days I'll teach the four of—"

Kandi cut him off by sprinting away in Eric's direction; she used her air to push her faster than she had ever run before, and it still took almost twenty-five minutes to reach where he had fallen to the ground unconscious. Instinctively she tried breathing air into his lungs, but it didn't seem to help, so she tried blowing on his heart to get it to pump more blood to his brain. Another few moments and he stirred. "Let go of the water you've got in the pipes!" Kandi screamed in desperation. "If you don't, it'll kill you!" She stayed there, kneeling, for what to her seemed like an hour, though it was only a little more than a minute, until Eric opened his eyes and groaned. He looked at her questioningly. "Using that much power for a long time drains you," she answered. "Don't try to get up until you get your strength."

Dega, Dru, and Barrett arrived as Eric, supported by Kandi, was attempting to stand. They made sure he was okay before agreeing that enough had taken place for one night.

The next day, they found that Barrett had recovered perfectly well with sleep, but Eric was still dazed, so it was decided that Eric would go with Dru to get the copper and the water pipes; he had measured how much they needed before he blacked out.

At breakfast, Blake asked about their absence, and Dega,—deciding so little of the truth could hurt nothing, replied, "After you went to bed we looked at the electrical and hydraulic conditions. They went to the city to the north and east of here for some things."

Lowell had to be talked out of contributing to that part of the restoration effort, and from there the daylight hours went just like they had the day before. They finished the church building and decided to start on a few houses the next day.

"So what are we doing tonight?" Dru asked.

"Let's put out the copper," Dega suggested. "Having electricity is more important than running water since we have all the bottled water."

The next two hours were spent cutting the copper into inch-segments and placing them. They had overestimated the distance they would need to go by two miles, which made them all pretty happy.

"Now watch," Barrett requested. He concentrated on the electricity already in the wires that hadn't been damaged and brought the current to the first piece of copper. He then took the current to the second piece, and the third, all the way to the end. When he finished, he noticed Kandi looking at him worriedly. Before she could comment, Barrett smiled and reassured her. "I'm not makin' electricity start from nowhere this time," he said. "All I did was move electrical particles. They keep themselves together. I'll be fine."

"Let's test it," Eric said.

"You doubtin' me, boy?" Barrett asked playfully.

"Every minute of every day," Eric replied, laughing.

They went back to the motel and flipped the light switch, filling the room with a non-natural glow that had escaped their vision for far too long.

"I guess you managed it." Eric said, and his comment was the last thing spoken before bed.

Morning arrived all too soon, and the five of them walked to the recently completed church building to find Lowell starting the breakfast fire outside. "Y'all've got electricity," Barrett told him. "We all stayed up late last night and got it back."

"Do what?" Lowell asked, sure he had misheard.

"Go turn the kitchen oven on," Dega said, backing Barrett up; they hadn't rebuilt the kitchen completely, but it hadn't been destroyed completely, either.

Kandi laughed at Lowell's expression. "It'll work! Go try it!"

Though obviously hesitant, Lowell complied. "I'll be," he muttered to himself. "How'd y'all do it?"

"Science," Barrett told him happily.

As Lowell continued to stare in amazement, shouts came from where Jacob and Blake were waiting. Dega looked worriedly at Lowell, and they all headed toward whatever scene was happening.

The first thing Kandi saw was a gun in Blake's hand. After that, nothing was very clear; it all ran together. She remembered hearing something about whose house to rebuild, Lowell asking Blake to put the gun down, false imprisonment, Barrett asking him to put the gun down, words too vile to repeat, a gunshot, a scream coming from Kandi's own mouth, Dega and Lowell running toward Jacob, Eric controlling a rod of ice to knock the gun away, Barrett holding Blake down.

Dega examined Jacob's wound. "Kandi!" he called her over but, noticing her standing motionless, realized she must have been in shock. He looked at Lowell. "Do you have a knife on you?" he asked quickly.

"Yeah." Lowell pulled his knife. "What's your plan?"

"Just watch." Dega took the knife and inserted it into Jacob's wound.

"*What are you doing?*" Lowell shouted, having enough medical knowledge to know that you never, under any circumstances, insert a dirty blade into a wound.

Dega ignored him, and eventually got the bullet out, though he made a bigger cut than he would have liked, but just the same he moved his hands over Jacob's body and healed him.

A few seconds later they both stood. Jacob started toward the still pinioned Blake, but Lowell took hold of his arm and restrained him. "You are *not* still breathin' for revenge."

Dega looked at Jacob, the look of vengeance still in his eyes, and then at Blake, the look of death in his. "This needs to be dealt with. Now." He looked at Dru, Kandi, Eric, Barrett, Robert, Ramona, and Ruby—the last three had run up upon hearing the gunshot—and made sure that they, simply from the look in his eyes, knew to keep quiet. "What is the problem between you two?"

"I just got a bullet in me!" Jacob cried, pulling slightly against Lowell's restraint.

Dega was not impressed. "I meant before that."

Again Jacob spoke. "I was put in jail for somethin' I didn't do and then treated worse than a dog by *him*."

"I was only following orders!" Blake responded, defending himself. He let his voice fall back to normal level before continuing. "I knew you didn't assault that guy; you had more to eat and more leniency than anybody else in there and were ungrateful for all of it."

Jacob seemed confused and defensively asked, "What are you talking about?"

"If they were starving, you were hungry. Things like that."

"Well then," Jacob's voice had a hint of sarcasm, "why didn't you let me out?"

"I had a family," Blake said, his voice quieter. "If I'd have let you go, I would've lost my job and paycheck. Surely you can appreciate that."

Jacob was silent for a moment. "I guess so. I can't forgive, and I won't forget, but I guess I at least understand."

Blake didn't respond, so Lowell spoke up. "Forgiveness is necessary, Jacob."

"But it doesn't always come easy," Dega said, looking at Lowell. He then turned to Jacob and Blake. "If both of you will at least stop hating each other, forgiveness will come. And even if it doesn't, at least peace will."

Neither spoke, but Dega read their minds and knew that they could at least stop their bickering.

"Good," Lowell said, sighing. "I'm glad that's settled. Dega, can I talk to you in the kitchen for a minute?" He turned to the others. "We'll be right back."

Dega knew what Lowell wanted, but still he followed until they were out of sight and hearing range of the others.

"I was blind to accept the healing of Blake. I dismissed it as a miracle. But I just saw a man, shot beyond recovery, healed within seconds. I also see the evidence of electricity being restored to a town by four teenagers and their teacher, by the light of the moon, no less." Dega was quiet. "Care to explain?"

Dega searched Lowell's mind and went over his options in his head. Lowell was a good man and he understood that some things in life simply had to be done, so he could probably keep the secret, but Dega still didn't want to reveal too much. "We all have obtained *powers,* meaning we all have control over something. Obviously, I have the ability to heal. Barrett can control electricity."

"If I hadn't seen it with my own eyes I wouldn't believe it. So what exactly are they?"

Dega breathed. "It's not sorcery, and its purpose is to stop the attacks."

Lowell stared at Dega for a long moment, but understanding he would get nothing more, he thanked Dega for telling him.

"Don't tell anyone else," Dega requested in a confident voice. "My friends probably don't approve of the little I've told you."

Lowell nodded. "Okay. Is there any way I can help?"

"Not right now. If that changes, I'll let you know."

The rest of the time they were in Oswego went as normally as it possibly could have. They finished rebuilding the houses of the survivors by day, and by night they fixed whatever they couldn't do without a power. It was only one small town, but, as it was the first time they had used their powers to help people, they felt like it was a precursor to what was to come.

CHAPTER 6

The five of them continued westward after leaving Oswego, crossing the Mississippi River the first day. The rolling hills were left behind, and the land leveled off, allowing them to see for miles, a fact none of them were too thrilled with. The landscape looked horrific. Everything, everywhere, was awful.

Decimation, destruction, devastation, desolation.

Obviously, there were exceptions, places that had been left alone, physically unscathed by the attacks. Sadness, misery, and dejection raged there.

Horrific.

They'd been driving less than a week and yet had seen more than any single person should be required to endure in a lifetime. They managed to find a map and tried to find some geographical pattern to the attacks but had had no luck. So they simply drove west, never staying in one place for more than an hour or two, save at night. They had come to the conclusion that if they continued to build back every little town they came to, tens of millions more would die.

They drove, found a place that had taken a direct hit, got

out, looked around for nothing in particular, left, drove, found a place that had taken a direct hit—to the point it became tedious.

A week after leaving Oswego, they came upon another decimated town. Even in the dense fog it looked small—not quite as small as Oswego but small enough to seem to Dru like there would have been nothing to do for fun, even before the attacks.

As had become customary, Dega stopped the van and they all exited. No one was in sight; everyone was either dead or smart enough to leave. They stood for a few moments before deciding to walk around to stretch their legs. They couldn't see well; all they knew was they were standing on grass in the midst of some buildings. Conversation flowed—they had become accustomed to horrid scenes such as this, but they still spoke softly out of respect for the dead—until they noticed a large sign on the edge of their vision. Dega was curious and walked closer, but when he read it, he stopped. Eric called to him, asking whether it told where they were. Dega didn't answer, and Eric, curious why he hadn't responded, walked over to ask again but quieted when he saw the sign. The other three eventually noticed, came near Dega and Eric, and stood in the same shock of realization.

The sign was a scoreboard.

They were standing on what remained of a high school football field.

No one was willing to break the silence of thought that surrounded them, nor did they want to. They all simply needed time to themselves and so dispersed.

His memories of only a few months earlier as a P.E. teacher took Dega straight to the gym. He was appalled to find that the

68

explosion was at a distance so close that everyone was killed but so far that the bodies weren't disintegrated completely. He couldn't make out features, but he could tell where warm bodies had been at the time of the strike. It seemed to be at least two classes of students and, he assumed, as many teachers. He felt sick seeing so many students who had died doing what he loved. He flashed back to his classes where students were happy to be able to release energy and enjoy themselves and, in some instances, let go of all the stress in their school and home lives.

Dega left the gymnasium and walked to find what used to be the baseball and softball fields, on which he had spent many years as a player and a coach. He viewed the damage to the fields momentarily but couldn't bear the weight of seeing his childhood in ruin and so returned to the school building. He looked in on a classroom. He could tell that no one had known what was happening; there were parts of corpses still resting in a few of the desks that had managed to survive the blast, and the teacher was still near the board. It was gruesome and Dega was extremely shaken. He went into his mind and took his concentration away from the school. Remembering his friends, he read their minds to see how they were handling this and found what he feared he would: they were just barely keeping their sanity.

The normally *I-don't-deal-with-details* Dru had tears streaking down her face as she slowly walked through what remained of the high school which, sadly, she was able to tell had been destroyed during the school day. She thought she had looked upon hundreds of teenage remains lying in the classrooms.

She came to a classroom which she immediately knew to be English, and her love of the subject drew her in. Tears still flowing, she tried to take in the scene before her. Beside a corpse to her right lay a book that resembled a journal. Scared of what she might read but unable to help herself, Dru picked it up. It was opened to a page dated only a week before.

I can't wait for Collin to pick me up tonight! He said he was going to take me to eat over in th

The entry ended, and Dru's tears turned to sobs.

Amazing, Barrett thought. He had ended up in what had obviously been the school's band room. He looked around at the destroyed instruments. He almost jumped when his eyes landed on the two sets of remains he hadn't previously noticed. *Everything in here, gone so quick*, he thought.

Back home, Barrett had been one of the saxophone players in the school band. It wasn't a large band, but when they played their school fight song and everyone cheered, cold chills ran up his spine. It was one of the best feelings in the world, and he was lucky enough to have experienced it.

Looking around again, he started thinking. Maybe he would never get to play in a band again. Maybe he wouldn't even so much as get to play again. Maybe—he cut himself off. *Maybes don't do nothin' but get you worried,* he chided himself. *Stop thin—* Again he stopped himself.

Maybe there wouldn't ever be another school fight song played.

Eric didn't bother moving from the football field; he went inside himself. He didn't know what was running through the minds of his companions, but, whatever it was, he hoped they were taking it better than he was. He didn't understand why it was hitting him so hard; it wasn't like this was the first destruction he'd seen. Maybe he was just emotionally unstable and delirious from lack of sleep. Whatever the case, he began to think about the students who used to attend the school, who used to live for what happened each Friday night. They had been worry-free, ready to take on the world. Most had probably been dating, some in a sport they had hoped to pursue for the rest of their lives.

The rest of their lives.

Eric could hardly take it. The ones who hadn't made it had missed *life*. They all had had dreams, none of them to be realized.

He started thinking about home. He'd known basically his whole school; there hadn't been anyone who was truly mean-spirited. They were all kids, naïve and oblivious to the large world outside their own. It's said that if you have one good friend in life, you've done well; Eric had had more than just one. He thought of them and wondered if they were okay. Just the thought made him more worried than he'd ever been. He knew that they were one of two things: living or dead. If living, then obviously it was a good thing; but if dead, he thought to himself, then at least they wouldn't have to see anyone else killed. But the thought still took a firm grip on him. It depressed him. All the things he had previously thought regarding the students of this school were probably true of his friends. They also had had their lives cut short. They'd been living good lives, not bothering anyone outside their own small worlds. They were dead for no reason at all.

Then again, he didn't know whether they were dead, and that got him even more worried.

And then it got him mad.

Eric usually wouldn't get mad. He was cool-headed and easy-going, trying to enjoy life no matter the circumstances. Even in the most difficult situations, he wouldn't get truly *mad*.

But he was now. There were people trying, for some unknown reason, to take the lives of his friends. They were wreaking all the havoc possible just so they could have whatever in the world it was they wanted. They were evil people who deserved a few bullets to the head. And so far, they were winning. Eric and Barrett and Kandi and Dru and Dega had been trying to find some way to stop them for naught.

Eric fell to his knees and began crying—truly crying, not just tearing. With all the emotion he was experiencing, he cried hard. He wanted to go home. He couldn't do it anymore; he needed Tennessee mountains about him.

But I can't, he thought. He had to stay. The five of them, plus one, would have to stay together. If they didn't, it was entirely possible that everyone would die. Everyone.

Even if that did eventually happen, Eric vowed his weakness would not be the cause.

He stayed on the ground crying for a few minutes before he was able to stand and see straight.

How did this become...this? Kandi asked herself silently as she walked around the debris on the football field. She laid her eyes on what looked to be a goal post and became lost in the memories of high school: staying up late for hours on the phone with her friend Bri, Kayla pushing her off the swing that day in kindergarten, spending time with her friends on the football team. She wouldn't miss a game; every Friday she showed up to support her team on the field. She looked at football as a different world in which a single second could determine victory or defeat. She lived for the adrenaline she felt as the players ran as fast as they could, trying to help the running back score the winning touchdown.

Now she looked upon the field with pain in her heart. She wondered where everyone was—the players, the band, the fans—and mentally contemplated whether they were dead or alive, wondered what Bri and Kayla and her other friends had been up to. An unwelcome feeling crept into her soul: homesickness. She wanted to see her friends and family. Where were Mom and Dad? Bradley? She regretted leaving them and wished she could go back in time to ensure that she never went that day with Dega. As she wished, she saw her mother's bright eyes in her mind's eye and wished she could really see them.

Instead, she saw where she was standing: a destroyed football field with an overturned goalpost. Suddenly a tear left her face and her emotion built inside her. At a loss, she just lay down on the field in a spot not covered in debris. The pain overran her, scaring her beyond belief. She wanted to know how her friends and family were. She wanted assurance.

"Kandi …" she heard a voice she recognized as Eric's say softly. A few seconds later she felt a hand on her arm. She didn't understand why he was attempting to comfort *her*; everyone was having a rough time—she knew they were. Then it occurred to her that she had, in fact, lain down and that she was silently dehydrating her body through her eyes. She went back to her thoughts and cried harder.

"Is she okay?" Kandi heard what she assumed to be Barrett's voice ask from a distance away. Eric must have silently signaled, because Kandi didn't hear a response. She felt Dru take her hand, and for a few long minutes Dru, Eric, Barrett, and Dega sat with their still-crying friend.

CHAPTER 7

For obvious reasons, they didn't stay much longer at the high school. They had no specific destination in mind; they simply went. The only thing they could do was drive to the next place that had been hit.

The fog had dissipated and the sun had come out—which lifted everyone's spirits somewhat—and the temperature had warmed. The scenery had changed; instead of the flatness that had surrounded them before, they had valley walls to each side. This was a great relief to Barrett and Eric; the road ran right alongside one of the mountains.

They were in silence for a long time after leaving the school, broken only when Dega began to feel a pain that seemed almost foreign to him; it took him a second to realize it was from Kandi's mind.

Hold yourself together, he heard her trying to control herself. *You knew this was what you were going to be seeing when you left out. Get yourself together! Don't cry, don't worry. Breathe. Think of a meadow with animals all around and—*

"Kandi, is everything alright?" Dega asked, interrupting her thoughts. From only those few words, Kandi burst into tears which no one, save Dega, understood.

"What's wrong?" Eric asked, concerned.

"I just need ... I just need a minute ... can we pull over?" Kandi asked, managing to get out and trying to catch her breath.

Dega complied. "Okay, we're just going to walk in that direction. We'll leave you here as long as you need. If you need any of us, just yell." He looked at Kandi for a second. "Are you gonna be alright?" Kandi nodded her head confidently. "Okay then," Dega turned and looked at the rest of them, "let's go on and give her some time."

"Hey, what's wrong?" The voice startled Kandi; her friends hadn't been gone that long, and she hadn't thought there was anyone else nearby.

"You are...?" Kandi asked, still somewhat dazed.

"Aimee," the stranger replied simply.

"I'm Kandi." She was still wary of her visitor.

"Why are you crying?"

Kandi tried to bring herself under control before responding. Failing, she answered, "If you had seen what I did at a high school a few miles back, you would be crying, too. If you haven't noticed, *everybody* is under attack and no one seems to have any answers."

Aimee half-laughed. "Oh, believe me. I've noticed." Her voice had grown somewhat weaker. "That's why I'm out here; I'm actually from southern California. Downtown L.A. and the naval base in San Diego were both hit and pretty much destroyed. I was living on the outskirts of L.A. and could feel the explosion."

"That doesn't come close to really knowing what's going on!"

Kandi exploded. "Have you seen the deaths of hundreds of teenagers and their teachers? Have you seen how obvious it is that people have no idea what's about to happen to them?"

"Yes and no. I have seen buildings and houses that had been destroyed. I didn't see the dead people up close, but I knew it existed."

Silence filled the space between them while Kandi calmed down some and processed what Aimee had just told her.

"Is that what brought you here?" asked Kandi.

"I had to get away. It was too awful, even for me. I've been out here before, so I knew where to come."

"How have you survived out here?" asked Kandi.

A semi-grin appeared on Aimee's face. "Would you like to see my hideout?" she offered.

Kandi hesitated. This Aimee was someone she had never met before; for all she knew, Aimee could be in with the terrorists. But at the same time, the sincerity with which she spoke about the missiles seemed real enough. Kandi thought a moment more. "Sure." Then she remembered her friends waiting on her. *Mr. Talladega will be able to find me.* "I'll go."

"I'm worried about her," Dru finally said. They hadn't walked more than two minutes before reaching a small pond that seemed to extend right into the wall of the mountain. It looked soothing, so they had all sat down beside it.

"Me too," agreed Eric. "Y'all think of anything can be done to help?"

"Just be there for her and listen if she needs to talk," Dega said, though he sounded far away— however hard he tried to conceal it. "That's just all we can do."

"I understand where she's coming from," said Dru. "I'm still a little emotional."

They were quiet for a few seconds, so a curious Barrett took the opportunity. "What's on your mind, Mr. Talledega?"

He seemed almost hesitant to answer but conceded and said, "I actually don't know. There's something odd messing with my power."

Dru got obviously nervous. "Do you think the people we're after know about us and how to fight it?"

"Unlikely," said Eric. "The ones who came before us have gone down in history as myth, and I can't see somebody not believin' that's exactly what they were."

"I agree," said Dega. They waited for him to say more, but he remained silent.

Around ten minutes passed with Eric and Barrett longingly looking at the scenery before Dru said, "I think we should go back." She hadn't liked leaving Kandi alone in the first place, though she understood it to be necessary and knew that Kandi could defend herself quite well.

No one verbally agreed or disagreed; they all just stood and began walking back in the direction from which they had come. When they were close—though still out of sight—Dega got a worried expression on his face and began to run; the other three wisely kept up. Dega was the first one there and, when he didn't see Kandi, checked inside the van, though he knew it useless, and then shouted her name a few times. Eric got there a few seconds later. "What?" he asked worriedly, knowing Dega would understand the rest of the question.

"I don't know," Dega told him.

Eric's voice started to get louder. "Where is she?"

"Again, I don't know."

"Well, use your Pow'r and *sense where she is!*"

Dru and Barrett arrived as Dega replied, "I'm just as worried as you are; there's no need to yell. I don't know why, but I'm not able to sense her."

Barrett was the only one to still completely have his head about him. "Is she too far away?"

Dega took a breath before answering. "No, we weren't gone long enough for that. Something is … clouding my power. I can barely sense you."

"*Clouding?*" Dru asked.

"I don't really care what *clouding* is," Eric said, controlling his voice. "Let's just go find her real quick."

"I was about to say the same thing," Dega said. "Me and Dru will go up this way, the two of you that way."

"If we find her," Barrett added, "we'll yell. You should be able to hear us. No matter what, we all come back here in an hour and a half."

"No," Dru said. Everyone looked at her.

"Why. Not." Eric's words were almost threatening.

Dru gathered her thoughts. "We've actually lost Kandi. We may or may not get her back, but as of now we've lost her. We need to stay together."

The other three looked at each other, the silence lasting long enough to allow Eric to calm himself. "Is it really that important to you?" he asked. Dru nodded.

"Then let's get goin'," said Barrett. "We've got twice as much ground to cover now."

The mountain they chose to trek first—the one nearer them—was a dense forest of trees, with parts of the ground coming up higher than they should have and parts sinking lower. The group walked level with each other across, with about fifty yards in between each of them to better search the unwelcoming landscape. They alternated calling her name for a while, but then Barrett made the point that, were she within hearing range, she would have already heard and responded. The rest reluctantly agreed and kept quiet.

After searching for about forty-five minutes—none willing to be the first to say that maybe they wouldn't ever find her— Dru called for Eric, Barrett, and Dega. They obliged and stared at the five-by-four-foot opening in the side of the mountain as Dru asked, "What do you think?"

"I think somebody'd better get us some light," Eric said, "'cause it's pretty dark down there."

"I got it." Dru created a flame that levitated in her hands.

"Still dead set on stayin' together?" Barrett asked.

Dru once again nodded her affirmation, and she led the search party into the cave. It was completely dark aside from Dru's fire, so much so that it was hard to make out even the floor. Barrett asked if she could make it brighter. "Not without blinding us," she answered.

"Cover your ears," Eric said right before he screamed out Kandi's name.

Echo, echo, echo, silence. No reply.

More than once someone tripped over something they hadn't seen on the ground, and the cave got so wide that they spread out across again so that they would trip over a body they couldn't see, were there one.

"How much farther sh—" Dru started to ask when she heard a loud splash. Scared, she looked to her right but didn't see Eric. Again she started a question, "Wha—" and was cut short by another splash, this one much louder than the first, from which emerged Eric, shivering and gasping for breath.

"Don't move!" he said quickly. "I fell into a lake; it completely surrounds our path here, meaning if anyone takes another step, you'll fall in." He stopped talking for a second and sent the water droplets from his clothes back into the water. "The land in this tunnel ends here; we have to go back."

Dega was the only one brave enough to voice the question. "She's not …?"

"I don't know, and I'm not sure I could even find out."

"Then let's go back into the sunlight," Barrett said.

They formed a straight line this time—they weren't busy searching—and no one stumbled at all.

Back outside, Barrett said, "You don't even have a little bit of water on you; I know you can control it, but still, that's unnerving." Eric semi-smiled.

They started back searching the mountainside as they had been, and it wasn't long before Barrett said, "Oh no."

"What?" Dru asked.

"Another cave."

Dega spoke. "With these two so close together, I think it's safe to assume there are hundreds. We can't search through them all, so let's make that a last resort and for now keep scouring in the open." No one disagreed.

For about half an hour they kept at it like that, until Eric saw a sheet of rock that seemed to extend straight up; the farther up he looked, the more it extended away from the mountainside. The sides of it went back until they met with the ground again. This wasn't the first he'd seen like it, but as he neared it he began to feel different. He didn't know what it was, but he actually felt *good*. He couldn't understand why he felt like this, considering they were looking for their lost friend. Then it dawned on him. "Hey, y'all come look at this!" he yelled. The other three ran toward him as quickly as they could.

"It's just a big rock wall," Dru said. But as she neared, he saw a smile of understanding come upon her face.

The same happened to Barrett. "My power feels stronger," he said simply. "She's gotta be in there."

"How do we get in?" Dega asked, looking almost with awe.

"Some kind of trap door?" Eric suggested.

"You don't honestly think there's something that opens in something as solid as that?" Dru asked.

"No, but I *really* don't believe you could just walk right through the thing as if it weren't there."

Nobody said anything as they mentally evaluated what Eric had just said. Barrett finally went up to the wall and walked as if to go through. His head hit the stone and he let out a slight groan. "I whole-heartedly agree with you," he said, head in hands.

They began to look for a trap door in the wall or anything that would make it open. Once or twice Dru thought she had something, but nothing worked. They knew Kandi was in there; they just didn't know *how* she'd gotten in there.

While the others continued, Dega decided to try to see if there was some kind of entryway in the side of the wall. He hadn't gone more than thirty yards up the mountain when he noticed a spot of brush that seemed to have been trampled. He called the others over and they found an entrance into the rock. This time Barrett, remembering he could also make a light source, went first. The four of them—two functioning lanterns and all—hadn't gone down more than ten yards before the tunnel curved up and deeper into the mountain. Another fifty and it sloped downward again, but as they took that slope they noticed a light from around a bend ahead. They took the curve, and Barrett and Dru extinguished their lights. There was, somehow, plenty of sunlight; the tunnel must have curved farther than they had realized. In the sunlight, Dru saw Kandi, but she saw her twice; there were *two* Kandis. It was obvious to

Dru which was the real one—the softer eyes gave her away—but aside from that it looked like an actual clone. Kandi and Kandi-Number-Two stood there looking at Dru, Dega, Eric, and Barrett for all of a second before the clone sprinted down farther into the tunnel almost faster than the rest could see. It stunned the guys somewhat, but Dru instantly ran and swung her arms around Kandi. "Are you okay? And who was that?" she asked.

Eric, Barrett, and Dega had managed to shake off their paralysis and get over to the girls by the time Kandi answered. "Her name was Aimee. Right after you guys left, she came down to me and asked why I was crying. I told her everything that had happened, and she felt sorry for me. Long story short, she convinced me that if I came with her, no one would find me. She said she'd been living out here for weeks and camping out here all her life. She said it's perfectly safe, and I wouldn't ever have to endure anything like that again. I shouldn't have come up here, I know it, and I'm sorry, but I was emotional and not thinking straight, and then I realized it was like looking into a mirror which confused me even more ..." Kandi said, starting to cry.

"Yeah, what was with that?" Barrett asked softly, moving closer to her.

"I don't know."

"I do," Dega chimed in. "Right before she ran off I read her mind, and just now—forgive me, but I had to—I looked into yours. Both your earliest childhood memories and hers are identical. The two of you are twins."

"We're *what?*" Kandi asked, astounded.

"You have your power back?" Eric asked, not able to resist his curiosity.

Dega looked at Eric. "I figured out what the problem was and got around it." He turned his gaze back to Kandi. "You are exactly what I told you: twins. To make things even more interesting, the reason that I didn't run right after her when she took off is that she has the last power, earth. She could easily manipulate the tunnels to trap whoever she wanted in here, so we'll just have to catch her later. The unknown presence of the sixth power was blocking me from reading minds."

They were quiet for a minute—Kandi had let up crying—before Dru asked, "Why did she run?"

"While the four of you were being held by your shock, something happened, but only Aimee and me had enough self-awareness to feel it. The six of us were together! Our powers were the strongest they can ever be! Aimee had no idea what was happening, so her first instinct was to run."

"How will we find her?" Kandi asked slowly.

"I read her mind," Dega answered. "I think I know where she might run to."

CHAPTER 3

Barrett tried to look around, to familiarize himself with his surroundings, but he didn't notice much; rather, he noticed the *absence* of much. The buildings still stood, since this wasn't near where any missile had hit, and some people walked past every now and then. But to the eye of anyone who looked, it was obvious something had gone horribly wrong in this place. He could hear birds, but that proved the point: you shouldn't be able to hear birds over the usual noise from the outskirts of L.A. "What makes you so sure she came back here?" he asked.

Dega turned away from the shoreline to face Barrett. "I'm not overly sure," he admitted, "but this is the only place we know about, so we might as well check."

Eric spoke up. "I still can't believe it's a loadin' dock."

"Why not?" Kandi asked.

Eric shrugged. "Just seems a little odd for a hang-out spot, especially with everything that usually goes on there in movies," he said. Kandi shook her head.

"Secluded," Dru said, almost longingly. "Loud. Out of the way. I'd be surprised if a lot of people didn't use them."

Eric raised his eyebrows and nodded, conceding the point.

As they walked, the sky gradually began to darken; they'd had to abandon the van both to keep the tires from the damaged roads and to avoid speculation that would surely come were they to drive the empty streets. Barrett had a thought. "What are we gonna do if we can't convince her she needs to stay with us?"

"Play it by ear?" Dru suggested.

"No, Barrett's right," Kandi said. "We do need a plan."

"Talk to her," Eric said simply.

"But I'm sayin' what if that doesn't work?" Barrett repeated.

"Keep her here and keep talkin' to her. Reason is the only way to 100 percent get her to work with us. We'll figure it out." By then they had gotten close. "Is she here Mr. Talladega?"

"There's no way to tell without reading the minds of everyone here, something I'm not willing to do when we can just as well search with our eyes."

"Isn't that more dangerous?" asked Kandi.

"Yeah, but it's what we would do if my power were something else. I'm not gonna invade people's privacy for just anything."

No one was really willing to be the first to speak after that, so Dega said, "We're here. Do you wanna spread out or stay together?"

"Spread out," Eric, Barrett, and Kandi agreed, everyone still walking.

Dru tried to keep silent, but Dega just looked at her until she spoke. "I think we should stay together."

Just then they heard a loud bang, and a bullet whizzed past their heads. Immediately they scattered, jumping behind crates and out of sight. Then more shots could be heard; it sounded like whoever was shooting had switched to automatic. Barrett crept to an opening between his crate and the one next to it; it was just big enough to see out from. He thought he heard a few bullets whiz above his head, which was highly possible since he had the gunman in open sight. Barrett conjured up a ball of Electricity so powerful that the stranger would be obliterated and let it—

"*Stop!*" came a shout. It caught Barrett so off-guard that he momentarily obeyed. His electric ball that was once full of strength dropped to just enough voltage to knock out their enemy, and this time he did let it go.

The shooting stopped. Barrett saw no one of his party until Dega stood and walked over to the darkly-clothed gunman. He had an unknown crest on his sleeve, but Dega thought it unimportant and so hardly noticed. The other three plus Barrett followed. "Who was it?" asked Kandi, obviously shaken.

"The only thing I was able to get out of him before Barrett hit him was that he knew exactly who we were, and he was supposed to kill us," Dega told her while he took away all the man's weapons.

"He *what?*" Dru asked in disbelief.

Dega remained silent.

"Can't you look into his mind now?" Barrett asked. "I just knocked him out."

"His thoughts are too jumbled for anything much. We'll have to wait until he comes to."

"Oh." Barrett thought a second. "Who screamed *stop*?"

They were quiet until Dega motioned and said, "Her."

Aimee ran up and dropped to her knees beside the unconscious man and checked for a pulse. "Is he all right?"

"Should be," Barrett said cautiously. "I think I just knocked him out."

Aimee didn't even seem to be listening; she just appeared worried over the still unnamed man.

"Care to explain?" Kandi asked her sister.

Aimee kept her gaze directed down but answered. "After I—" she said, stopping herself. It seemed to dawn on her what was happening. She stood, positioning herself somewhat protectively over him, and started again. "After I ran away from you guys, I started to think about where I should go. This is Trevor; we ... have been friends for a long time." She paused. "I feel safe with him, so here we are."

"I'd just *love* to know why we were being shot at," Eric said somewhat sarcastically.

"I don't know!" The question obviously had upset her. "We saw you coming a few minutes before you got here, and he told me to go and hide. I just assumed he was gonna talk to you, so I stayed put. Then he pulled the gun ..."

Eric looked at Dega, who noticed his silent question and nodded that Aimee was telling the truth.

"Aimee, you can't run away this time," Dega said, changing the subject. "You have to stay with us."

"I don't think I do," Aimee responded, almost defensively.

Dega sighed and explained that her abilities with earth that had seemed unnatural were actually a power, and then he told the basics of everything they knew. Aimee seemed confused. "What are you gonna do to Trevor?" she asked, piecing together the fact that she couldn't save him from their wrath.

"Question him," Eric said. "We'll go from there."

Aimee looked at Dru, with her hard and unreadable expression; then at Barrett, who seemed ready for whatever was next; at Eric, with his calm look of assurance; Dega, looking older and wiser than his years; and last at Kandi, who was looking longingly back. "Okay," she said, nodding, "I'll stay with you."

"He'll wake up in a minute or two," Barrett told them, motioning at Trevor.

"Let's go over to the side of that building so he can't try to run." Dega said, more as a statement, but he kept his eyes questioningly on Aimee. She nodded, and Eric and Barrett carried Trevor to where Dega had suggested.

"When did you two meet?" Kandi asked Aimee while they waited for Trevor to come to.

Aimee answered without hesitation. "Six years ago on the bus to school. He was a few years older, so we didn't have classes, but we'd always sit next to each other and talk."

"Oh," Kandi replied. She was scared she would have to think of something to say so it wouldn't be awkwardly silent, but she was saved by the twitch of Trevor's head. He looked up at them, and for the first time Kandi noticed his features. He was average height with long legs and a short torso, and his face seemed to Kandi to be too handsome to be an enemy.

A quick look of understanding flashed across his face. "They'll come for me."

Dega ignored that and asked, "Why were you shooting at us?"

Trevor trained his eyes on Dega. "Because I was told to."

"And why were you told to?" Dru asked as Trevor stood up next to Aimee.

"I don't know."

Dega kicked the back of Trevor's knee out from under him and loudly said "*Liar!*" as he fell.

"What do you mean *liar*?" Trevor asked, once he'd wiped the dirt from the side of his face. "I told it like it is." He refrained from standing.

"You left out the part about working for the terrorists!"

Trevor's eyes slanted. "How did you know that?" he asked carefully.

"Don't worry about it. Just know that lying or leaving things out won't be good for your health."

It was obvious Trevor was more annoyed than scared.

For the first time, Aimee spoke. "Come on, Trevor ..." she said, almost weakly.

He looked at her, then back at Dega. "Okay, yes, I'm with *the terrorists* as you call us. Usually I'm not the one carrying out jobs like this because I'm up the political ladder somewhat, but ... " he said, hesitating. "But because of my connection to Aimee, I was sent." He waited for a response, but Dega just stared at him. "I knew you had some kind of abilities that allowed you to do things other people can't because that's the reason they want you dead, but I didn't think you could stop me if I had a gun," he said. Trevor half-chuckled. "And did I mention that my people will be coming for me?"

Aimee looked like she was about to burst into tears, so Barrett put his arm around her.

"There, doesn't it feel better to tell the truth?" Dega asked.

"What are we gonna do to him?" Eric asked.

Dega leaned down toward him so neither Trevor nor Aimee could hear. "For her sake and some leverage I say we keep him. Right now we need to have him and Aimee both guarded while the rest of us wait for them to show up."

"Sounds like a plan," Eric responded.

Dega went to tell Kandi and Dru quietly (Eric assumed Barrett would be fine with it, and he was too close to Aimee to be able to tell) and then said out loud, "We've decided that while three of us wait for *your people* to come, one will guard you and the other Aimee." Aimee looked a little surprised but accepted it in silence. Dega continued. "I was thinking Barrett would watch Trevor, and Dru can keep an eye on Aimee?"

No objections. Dru and Aimee went into the building they were standing by, while Barrett led Trevor to the one opposite. "You must be the one that shocked me," Trevor assumed out loud.

"Yeah, and I'll do worse if you don't behave."

Still outside, Dega, Eric, and Kandi looked around. "There's nowhere that really pops out as a good spot where we can all hide," Eric noted.

"Could we just wait in the open?" Kandi asked. "We can take 'em whether they see us or not."

"I think we should probably hide," Dega told her. "Just in case."

"Do we trust Aimee enough to have her make a place underground for us?" Kandi asked, though when she saw the looks on her companions' faces she withdrew her comment, saying, "Just a thought."

Eventually they noticed that there were two crates strategically placed near Dru's hideout with Aimee. Dega and Kandi went behind one, and Eric the other. They waited.

It was past midnight when Dega sensed the minds of their enemies. He quietly passed it on to Kandi, who then told Eric by whispering and making a small air current carry her voice. He stuck out his hand and gave a thumbs-up. Dega raised his eyebrows at the trick, and Kandi had to keep from laughing.

Eric stepped out in the open just long enough to let Dega see him point as his head. Dega got the message and read his mind. *Do we kill or capture?*

Dega thought for a moment, making a decision he'd never had to make before, then leaned to Kandi and said, "Tell Eric, *kill unless they're unarmed.*" She obliged.

Eric looked for the coming enemy but saw no one. He tried to listen for a car. Nothing. But then he heard something: splashing. He turned his gaze away from the direction they had come and to the shoreline. At first he saw nothing, but before long his eyes detected motion.

Four decent-sized dinghies were just barely visible in the

moonlight. As they approached, Eric hoped to himself that they wouldn't arrive shooting. He didn't want to kill; he would if he needed to, but he didn't want to. And yet, when he saw them dock, the first thing they did was retrieve heavy guns from the bottom of the boat. Kill.

Twenty-eight of them walked slowly toward the place where Eric was hiding; it was as though they knew exactly where they were going. Eric regretted that he hadn't checked Trevor for a tracker. As they got close, Eric braced himself.

A wind came out of nowhere. It started small but then grew into a strait wind that was so strategically placed it threw someone into the air, smashing his neck against the edge of a roof, instantly snapping it. The men were obviously caught completely by surprise.

Eric knew it was his turn. He summoned a cone-shaped area of water, froze it, and threw it right into someone's heart. He, too, died instantly.

Dega's voice came booming from a roof above. "Put down your weap—" They immediately started firing in the direction of the voice. Then Eric noticed that one of the men was grabbing at his throat before doubling over and being still. Kandi must have cut off his air supply. Eric was about to attack again when he felt a sting of bullets running through his leg. He wanted to cry out in pain, but instead he turned his head and filled the lungs of the four men who had found him with ice-cold water. They managed a small cough before they fell. Eric barely heard when Dega's voice again called for them to surrender from one of the roofs. Just as they had the first time, the enemy fired at it. By this, Eric knew they wouldn't surrender, and he also knew he was losing too much blood. He crept to the side of the crate just in time to see another three men right on him; he barely had time to make a sheet of ice to decapitate them all.

He was losing strength fast. There were only ten left—Kandi must've gotten the others—so he made ten small ice-pebbles, lodging one in the heart of each. They fell, and Dega sprinted over to Eric. The pain in Eric's leg lessened, but when Dega was done, there was still an intense sting pinpointed in his calf. "You missed a spot," Eric said through gritted teeth.

"The bullet's lodged in there," Dega responded. "The others went right through you, so I could heal those, but I can't take out the bullet."

"Meaning …?"

"I probably can," Aimee said. Kandi must've retrieved the others.

She was still about twenty yards away, so Eric whispered, "Can she?"

Dega was silent a moment, then replied, "Physically, yes. She doesn't intend to hurt you. But her intentions could change when she notices how she has you at her mercy."

By then, Dru and Aimee had arrived. The latter hesitated before she spoke. "…Something happened a few years ago, and I had to learn really quickly how to remove bullets."

Dru saw the look on Eric's face. "I trust her," she said as Barrett and Trevor joined.

The stunned look on Trevor's face when he saw the bodies interrupted the conversation.

Dega looked at him. "Just keep this little memory at the front of your mind. And know that this was done by our … nonoffensive powers."

"Go for it," Eric said to Aimee.

She looked around and picked up some sort of tool, though Eric couldn't see quite what it was. "This will hurt," she said as she kneeled next to him, all eyes on her. It didn't start bad, but after a few seconds, Eric found himself struggling to resist the urge to cry out. A little over a minute and he felt part of his skin being pulled away from him, and then his bone was exposed to air. As quickly as he could, Dega healed the opening. Eric stood and was, as always, surprised he could put weight on it. He turned to Aimee. "Thanks."

"Anytime."

As she said that, Barrett and Dega started sprinting toward the coast, the rest feeling it wise to follow. "What is it?" Kandi asked when they caught up.

Barrett was looking at a shape getting gradually smaller across the water. "Trevor. I took my eyes off him to watch Aimee take out the bullet, and he was gone. He hot-wired a speedboat that was docked here." Barrett looked at Eric. "Can you make the water swallow him?"

Eric looked at it and remembered Oswego. He shivered. "Too much distance."

Kandi looked at Aimee. "She didn't know," Dega said.

They stood there, silent and motionless, looking across the sea.

CHAPTER 3

After the boat had gone out of sight, it seemed to truly dawn on Aimee what had happened. She had run from the others, wanting freedom from this nightmare, wanting to never have to acknowledge it, wanting everything back to normal. When she finally couldn't breathe, she collapsed, crying hysterically and rocking back and forth. She wanted to cease existing, to fade into nothingness. Her world was collapsing around her, and she was helpless and alone. Nothing could help; no one could change anything.

It was approaching dawn before Dega told Kandi she could go to her. It took a few minutes to reach her, and when she finally did she seated herself on the dirt next to Aimee. Aimee was still crying, but it was noiseless; she had quit rocking. She had obviously noticed her presence, but neither said anything until the sun began to come up and Kandi spoke. "I'm sorry about your friend."

Aimee took her time responding. "Why did he ... ? I want to understand."

Kandi wasn't sure what to say to that, so she tried to evade the question by saying, "Mr. Talladega can answer that better than I can. How are y—"

"Where is he?" Aimee asked. She stood up suddenly, strengthened by her burning desire for the knowledge—and knowledge only. She looked down questioningly at Kandi.

Kandi returned her gaze nervously before also standing. "He's back where you found us," she answered. Aimee started walking, and Kandi followed. "Do you wanna talk about it while we're walking?"

"No," Aimee replied. Kandi could do nothing but follow in silence, hoping Aimee was okay.

"Hey," Dru said softly when Aimee was passing her, though "Where's Dega?" was the only reply she received. Dru pointed toward the bodies of the dead, and Aimee started in that direction. Dru looked at Kandi, who sighed and shook her head in response as they followed.

Dega, Barrett, and Eric were looking at the corpses when Aimee first saw them. "Why?"

Dega looked at her. "Which part?"

"Trevor shooting and running away."

Dega thought for a moment. "I've already explained to you about our powers, right?"

"Yes," she said with an absence of emotion.

"And you obviously know about the terrorist attacks. Our powers came to us because they are the only things that can stop the attacks. If we die, then they're fr—"

"I know that," Aimee said, interrupting. "I meant 'Why were you being shot at by *Trevor*?'"

Dega decided to make it quick and blunt. "He's in with them. It's not like he's a hired hand; I think he might actually have a voice and some power in deciding what's done. He knew he needed us dead, so he tried."

Aimee looked ready to start crying again. "Would he … " Her voice trailed off, and Dega thought this might be a good time to read her mind so she wouldn't be subjected to having to voice something so unpleasant. *Would he have killed* me?

"I don't know whether he would have or not," Dega told her quietly.

"And he ran away because he's in too deep?"

"He ran because he is one of them and it's what he wanted to do."

Aimee silently held her composure but looked devastated. Kandi reached a hand toward her, and, when she didn't object, hugged her. "Are you okay?"

Aimee looked misty-eyed when she replied. "No, but life goes on. I cried enough last night. And what you said yesterday about me not running away—I won't. I want to see him again."

"Glad to hear it," Barrett told her with a smile.

"Could you help us with this, then?" Eric asked her.

"Depends on what *this* is."

"We can't well leave the bodies right here—"

"—and you want me to make a mass grave. Yeah, I can help." She looked around. "Anywhere you would suggest?"

Dega answered. "We found a little hill just around the corner of the building over there."

"How are we going to move them?" Aimee said suspiciously.

"I have an idea," Kandi said. "It might not work, but I would think earth should be able to move the flesh and bone while water should be able to move the liquids, so if you worked together you might be able to do it."

Eric looked at Kandi. "First the wind carrying your voices, and now how to move bodies … " He laughed. "Is this what you think about when the rest of us are asleep?" he asked. Kandi smiled.

"Let's try it," Aimee agreed, her voice still emotionless. She closed her eyes and focused on the parts of the bodies that were solid, on the dust base of it all, and willed that it move. Eric did likewise with the liquids. The corpses began to shift across the ground slowly, and the two of them followed until they made it to the hill. When they stopped, Aimee almost fell, and Eric did drop to a knee before he regained his footing.

"Do you need a minute before you dig?" Dega asked.

"No," she said. "We didn't get tired. It was just the shock of stopping so suddenly from doing something that *should* have gotten us tired, I think." Eric nodded his agreement.

"Well that's new," Dega said, wonderingly.

Aimee looked at the hill. She could move the dirt off the top and then re-cover, but that was too close to the air for her to feel safe doing, so she dug a tunnel from the base down into the earth. She looked at Eric, and they put the dead into the hole before Aimee filled it. She added the excess dirt to the top of the hill, as it was grassless to begin with. She looked back at the others, somewhat pleased with her performance. "Now what?" she asked.

Dru answered. "I vote we go find a place to sleep." No one was against it, so they went back down the road to the van and drove to what was a mostly intact motel. Dega told them that he wanted some time to think before he slept and excused himself while everyone else stayed together.

Barrett spoke, almost solemnly. "Do y'all realize we could've been killed? And that would've been the end of us. Mr. Talladega can't do anything for us if we're already dead."

"Yeah, but that didn't happen so we shouldn't worry about it," Kandi said quickly, disliking the thought of it. "Let's just deal with what actually happens."

"I didn't come with you guys to be almost killed," Dru told

them. "I'm here to stop the attacks. We almost died without coming anywhere close to actually doing that."

"Dru," Eric said calmingly, "remember what Mr. Talladega's been sayin'. We've gotta be patient and eventually we'll understand."

"You knew this was gonna be dangerous, with everything we've all seen," Barrett said, strengthening Eric's point.

"Yeah, but ... " Dru wasn't sure how she wanted to finish.

"But what?" Kandi asked her.

Dru took a long, deep breath. "I don't know. It just hadn't felt real before. I don't know how to deal with this."

"None of us do," said Barrett, trying to reassure her.

"Right now we'd better keep our thoughts on survival mode and not worry too much about what we don't know," Eric said, mimicking Kandi's earlier statement. "We just need to stay focused on what we're doin' and nothing else."

Aimee had been silent through the conversation until then. "I need some sleep," she said.

"Same," Kandi said.

Barrett nodded. "We'll see y'all in the mornin'," he told them before he and Eric walked into their room and quickly fell asleep.

CHAPTER 10

Eric looked out the opening of their hideout in the wooded area just outside the city. The day after they buried the bodies, two more armed men came for them. Before Barrett electrocuted them, Dega gained from them that they had wanted to see if inconspicuousness would work where numbers had failed—so they all decided it would be best to leave the city. For the past few days, the six of them had been sitting inside the hill that Aimee had carved from the inside out, trying to figure out the answers to some questions, trying to see if there was something that one of them had seen that could trigger an idea from someone else about something they'd missed. Eric now thought it a waste of time and energy; if there were some bit of information like that, surely Dega would have found it when he asked to search their minds. He had let them continue because he could think of nothing useful they could be doing, until he realized something. "Where are the terrorists?" he asked, not even trying to seem like he was sorry for interrupting the conversation that had been going on around him.

Dru stopped midsentence. "What do you mean?" she asked.

Eric searched for the words. "They have missiles—we saw

that back in D.C.—and they obviously have a lot of people. So, where are they?"

Barrett spoke up. "You know, come to think of it, those documents I got on my phone at the Air Force Base actually said that they weren't havin' any luck findin' them."

"Satellites haven't picked anything up?" Dru asked, amazed that this had yet to come up.

"No. At least, they *hadn't*."

"That is strange," Dega said. He looked over at the map they had set up with all the known places that had been hit, which they'd gotten off the Internet earlier.

Kandi did the same. "The only inconsistency the world over seems to be that the US is getting hit more than everyone else; aside from that it looks pretty evenly distributed."

"Yeah, but that's nothin' new, us gettin' the worst of it, so we can't well call that an inconsistency," Eric noted.

"Let's see." Kandi said and started thinking. "If I were a terrorist …"

Eric laughed and then turned to Aimee. "You *are* allowed to comment if you want," he told her kindly. "Since you hid for a while, what's your thoughts on where they might be?"

Aimee smiled and said, "Hiding yourself and hiding an organization are two very different things, but … " She thought for a second. "Siberia and northern Alaska are possibilities."

"Too cold," Barrett commented.

"Exactly," she told him, "meaning there's no one else there."

"It's possible," Dru said. "There's also the Outback and the Sahara."

"You're pretty much the only one that'd be able to survive in that heat," Eric said, "and that's not for natural reasons."

"Buildings with air conditioning."

"True …"

"One of these islands?" Barrett suggested, pointing at Oceania.

"Most are small with enough human habitation to prevent it," Dega told him.

"Most," Barrett said, defending his point.

They kept looking at the map until Eric said, "So basically, we've got five different possibilities coverin' literally hundreds of thousands of square miles and no reason to put one over the others, and there could be places we've not thought of."

"Awesome," Dru said sarcastically.

"I know, right?" Barrett mimicked.

"Well, where can we rule out?" Kandi asked.

"Oswego," Eric told her.

"Where?" Aimee asked.

"Just a town that had been pretty much wiped out by the attacks," Barrett explained. Aimee still seemed confused.

"Where else?" Kandi asked.

While the rest were thinking, Dega commented, "That's actually about it. For all we know they're in L.A. and the boats were just an attempt to make us think otherwise."

"Was there nothing in Trevor's mind?" Dru asked.

Dega frowned. "You know, I don't remember noticing anything. It might've been because I hadn't thought to look for it but still ..."

"Back to what I said earlier," Dru started, "why haven't satellites picked anything up?"

"I can't think of any reason why they wouldn't," Barrett told her. "Mr. Talladega, you got anything?"

"I'm about as blank as you are." He thought for a second and added, "Signal jammers?"

Eric spoke up. "They would completely disable a satellite, which I assume," he looked at Barrett for confirmation, "hasn't happened." Barrett nodded. "And even that's assumin' they could actually get to one satellite, much less all."

"I hate to ask this," Kandi started softly, "but do you think the government's involved?"

Barrett laughed. "Our government? There's a lot they do that's not right, but I don't believe we're such an ignorant people as to put mass murderers in office. Now, someone *else's* government? Not unlikely."

"But every country's been hit," Aimee said, confused.

"There are people elsewhere in the world that would even kill their own for power," Dega told her.

"Kandi's right, though," Eric agreed. "There's gotta be somebody in some high-up place somewhere that's able to hide this."

"Or they're extremely technologically advanced," Dru added.

"So, again, we have nothing," Kandi said, sighing.

"But we do know their mindset," Dega said. "They're obviously determined, and they're power hungry. They don't care what the cost is, so long as they get their wish."

"That hardly helps," Dru said.

"It tells us that they aren't about to be talked with sensibly."

"Are you sure?" Kandi asked. "I hate to think we've lost all hope of talk being an option." Aimee shifted uncomfortably.

"Mr. Talladega actually left out one thing they want," Eric told her. She didn't reply, so he simply said, "Us dead."

No one spoke for a very uncomfortable moment, after which Dru asked, "So what do we do? And I don't mean, like, I know we're going to look for them and try to end this, but how? We've figured out only one thing while we've been here, and that's that we know nothing."

"It would take too long to go search everywhere you guys said they might be," Aimee said, though almost questioningly.

"And I personally don't trust that our plane wouldn't get hit," Eric put in.

"We have to figure out something," Kandi said, getting exasperated.

"Do we?" Dru asked. "If we are the *Destined*, that means that we're *destined* to stop them, right?"

"That's not how it works," Dega told her. "Some effort on our part is required."

"So what do you suggest we do with our limited and nonexistent information?"

"The next guy that comes after us," Eric said, "Dega could read him."

"But we hid so that wouldn't happen," Aimee told him.

"Well, I guess we'll just have to un-hide then, won't we?"

"What are you thinking?" Kandi asked.

"We could somehow draw them in."

"Yeah, we got that," Dru said.

"We could just move back into town somewhere and let them think there's no reason for it," Barrett put in.

"Too suspicious," Eric said, thinking a second. "One of us could pretend to go in for supplies or something while the rest of us watch and wait."

"Who?" Kandi asked.

Aimee spoke up. "I'm willing." No one replied. "I know you don't trust me completely, but you never will unless you let me do something to earn your trust."

Barrett was the first to speak up. "That's fine with me."

Aimee smiled when no one dissented. "Okay, so what do I do?"

Aimee almost looked over her shoulder but thought better of it. No reason to seem like she was worried. Then she realized that, were she really going for supplies, it actually would be perfectly normal to be nervous. She looked behind her and saw only a middle-aged woman; she sighed in relief. It was only another half mile to the supply store where she was supposed to get paper and pens; this side of the city hadn't been that badly hit. She quickened her pace some. She wasn't *scared*, but her natural instinct for self-preservation had kicked in, and she could feel something wrong. She knew they must have been watching her. Back in the woods, they had all decided that there were people in L.A. looking to see if they would come back, but she also knew that her friends were near. *Friends*, she thought. Before she'd met Kandi, she'd been out by herself so long that, aside from Trevor, she had no one to call a friend. Now she didn't have Trevor, which depressed her, but she did have people who she knew were watching out for her. Whether they truly cared about her, she didn't know, but that could come later. The thought made her feel better, and time seemed to speed up as she made it to the store.

She walked into the dark building. "Hello?" she called. No answer. She turned on the flashlight she had brought and quickly grabbed what she had come for before setting a few dollars on the unattended cash register. Looters would probably end up with the money, but Eric and Kandi had convinced her that it wouldn't have been right to just take things without paying if they could help it. She left the store and began her walk back. Then she remembered something and turned around. The woman who had been behind her should have already passed the store, but she was nowhere to be seen. Aimee had to control her breathing when she realized that the lady might well have been some of the terrorists' eyes. She kept walking back at what was a somewhat normal pace, given the circumstances but then stopped and almost screamed before diving through the nearest window at the sound of multiple guns being cocked at once. One person got a shot off and she heard something break next to her, but no one else fired. She knew they were waiting for her to get up. One or two were probably coming toward her in case she didn't. She summoned her power and made little arrow points out of the ground outside that she could shoot into anyone who snuck up on her. She heard someone outside; he was getting closer. She readied her arrows and waited for him to be up close so she couldn't miss. When she was about to throw them she heard a voice say, "Let go of those things before you kill somebody."

She released her hold on the arrows. "Killing somebody was the idea, Dega." She stood up and wiped the dirt off her face before turning around. Kandi seemed to be flying up to a rooftop with Dru, Barrett, and Eric standing below. She picked something up from the roof and threw it down to those waiting, though it seemed to fall slower than it should have. Aimee looked at Dega. "The one who shot at me?"

"No, one of the others. There are four of them."

Aimee walked to where the first body had landed and looked at Barrett. "That one managed to get a shot off just as I was sending my Pulse to immobilize them. Sorry about that."

"Don't worry about it," Aimee told him. "How are we going to get them back to the woods?"

Eric had been listening. "Was there rope or anything in the store?"

Aimee nodded and went to get it. She turned on her flashlight and walked toward what she thought she remembered as the right section of the store. As she was looking for the rope, she got a strange feeling in the back of her mind that she should turn around, and did so just in time to keep from getting hit with a shovel. It struck the floor with a loud shriek, and she reached out in her mind for the arrows she had left outside a few stores down. They took more time than she had anticipated to reach her, and the man had the shovel back in the air ready to swing before being struck in the back all the way from the skull down to the rib cage. He let out a yell before crumpling to the ground, dead. Blood poured out, and Aimee could hardly bare to look at what she had done. Barrett was the first to reach her. "Are you okay?" he asked, worried.

Aimee nodded but didn't speak because she knew that, if she did, her voice would crack and she would start crying. Barrett put his arm on her shoulder as Dega and Eric got there and started to lead her away, but she saw something that caught her eye. She ran to the metal chains and grabbed what she thought would be enough. "What are those for?" Barrett asked her softly.

"Those four out there," Aimee motioned with her head.

"Unless you plan on hanging them, this won't be much help."

"You could electrify the part that's not touching them, and then if they try to squirm they'll be shocked," she said, trying to think of something.

"That's not quite how it works," Barrett told her, smiling, still keeping his voice quiet. "The best thing we can do is find the rope. It'll work better."

Eric figured Aimee didn't want to go back there, so he went himself to get the rope, and then saw a few wheelbarrows and grabbed those, too. He answered questioning looks with "I ain't about to be the one carryin' 'em back to the woods."

They walked back outside, and Aimee saw the unconscious men still lying on the ground. "Do they not care that their people are dying?" She tried to sound strong as she asked the question. "Are they ever going to stop sending people?"

"Eventually they will," Dega told her. "But not until they're sure *we* can't be killed like this."

They loaded the men into the wheelbarrows and headed back uneventfully, careful to secure the ropes tightly when they lined the terrorists up on the ground outside the hill. "What are you gonna ask them?" Dru asked Dega.

"I'll try to find out where their base is. Actually, I'll ask anything I can think of. It's been kind of inconvenient that we've had to kill the others so fast without being able to glean much from them."

"Yeah, *inconvenient* is the word for it," Kandi said nervously.

"You know what I mean."

Aimee looked at the unconscious bodies. "About how long until they wake up?"

"Maybe a few hours," Barrett told her. "When the gun went off, I put a little extra into it."

For most of the duration of that time, they sat around and talked about lighter things, but as the time went on it got increasingly awkward; there were so few nonhorrid things left to discuss, and those didn't seem right to talk about because of the more pressing matters, so it was a great relief when the first one stirred. He was dazed and tried to bring his hand to his head but, failing, blinked and looked around. He was a tall man with fair skin and blonde hair, such that Dru thought he should have been a magazine model. Dega spoke to him. "I'm Dega, and you're in trouble."

The man responded but in a language Dru didn't understand. It sounded very guttural, and that alone was enough to make her fear this man slightly more than the other three. He stopped speaking, and there was silence. Dru looked at Kandi, who was obviously just as confused as she was. Just as she was about to say something, Dega opened his mouth and spoke in the same tongue as the man. Whereas the words of the first were fast spoken, Dega's were slow and methodical; to Dru's ear, his accent seemed okay, but it was obvious he was putting some thought into it. Dru heard Dega finish off with the word *English*.

The man's eyebrows raised and he started again in the same language, but Dega cut him off and said, "I said that we would speak English."

He let out a defeated breath and complied. "I must know how this is, that you speak German."

Dega looked at him. "I have my ways."

Aimee was seated next to Dru and whispered, "How?"

Dru responded, "I have no idea."

"Whatever then are these *ways*, they are good," the man told Dega. He was obviously unsatisfied but unwilling to press the matter.

"Repeat what you told me just a second ago, so they'll know," Dega said, motioning to his companions.

He obviously didn't like it, but since he was tied up, he did so. "My name is Michael—" (Dru heard Mi-sha-el) "—and I ask that you release me."

"Ain't gonna happen," Barrett said to him.

Michael seemed perplexed. "I do not understand."

"What do you not understand?" Dru asked. "It was a simple enough *no*."

"No, I have only meant that I do not understand how he has spoken."

Eric and Barrett looked at each other and smiled.

Dega addressed Michael again. "Why should we let you go?"

"Already have you taken my guns. I am now to you no harm."

"You're a terrorist!" Dega said to him in disbelief. "In this country, terrorists have almost no rights. That in itself is enough reason not to let you go." One of the others, a tan man with dark hair, opened his eyes.

"You say *terrorist*; I say *correct aligned*. I am on the side that wins and with the people that win."

"I have to disagree with you," Dega replied. "Now, we have a few questions for you."

Michael seemed to be waiting on the first question and said, "It is not my place to say *no*." He motioned to his bindings.

Dega proceeded. "Your whole organization has a lot of people, right?"

"Yes, this is correct."

"And a lot a weapons."

Michael smiled. "You do not know the half."

"So, where do you keep it all?"

The smile left Michael's face. "I do not know. I have not needed to know and I have not been told. The only people that know are in chairs of power."

The second terrorist to wake had been listening and now shifted uncomfortably. Dega looked at the German speaker for a few seconds—Dru suspected to read his mind—and then Dega turned his gaze to the second. This one, also, started talking in a foreign language, but Dru thought she recognized it as a mix between Spanish and French. Dega responded to him in the same way he had to Michael, and then in English said, "And the rest of this conversation will be in English."

This one was different in that he didn't respond, so Dega started. "What's your name?" he asked.

Again, he didn't answer. Michael watched closely to see what would happen. "I said, 'What's your name?'" Dega was clearly getting annoyed, so he said, "Okay, Arnau, would you like a different question?" His mouth and Michael's both dropped in surprise.

Arnau spoke, his English much more advanced than Michael's. "I don't see how you knew my name."

"And I don't see why you didn't bother to reply when I asked, so I guess that makes us even."

"We want each other dead, and I thought talking would be pointless considering that you'll probably kill me anyway."

"We may, we may not," Dega replied. Arnau again was silent. "Michael just said that he doesn't know where your base is. Would you happen to know?" There was a hint of sarcasm in Dega's voice.

"Do I know? Yes. Will I tell you? No. That would not be beneficiary to our cause."

"You know," Dega said, looking up at the sky as if thinking, "I think you are going to tell us."

"And why is this?"

"Because we don't like it when people try to kill our friends," Dru answered.

Arnau picked up Dega's sarcastic tone. "My apologies to the young lady," he said, with a slight bow of the head to Aimee.

Dru's hand suddenly caught fire, such that Aimee had to move away a little. Arnau eyed it suspiciously. "Watch it, Dru," Dega warned her.

"Why?" Dru asked, directing her question to Dega but keeping her eyes on Arnau. "I think this'll work just fine."

Arnau smiled. "The six of you are too *good* to torture me—" saying the word *good* in a mocking tone. "So again I say that I will not reveal our location," he continued. "This conversation is meaningless."

By the time Dega realized what was going to happen, Dru had already unleashed her flame. It hit Arnau in the left leg and did nothing but burn for a few seconds—until Kandi was able to grab her and Eric could douse the blaze. Dega was about to heal the now screaming Arnau until he saw Barrett pointing at his own head. *Heal a little, and offer to finish if he tells us where.* Dega thought that somewhat unethical, but considering the circumstances, he went along with it.

Arnau's screaming became reduced to whimper-like sounds and the occasional groan, and through gritted teeth he said to Dega, "Help me." It seemed a struggle for him to get the words out.

"Not until you tell us where it is."

"No!" His tone seemed to be convincing, though whether it was for his own benefit or that of his hearers Dega didn't know.

He started screaming again, and Dru said, "Some things have to be done, Mr. Talladega."

"Dru!" Michael was the one to yell this time.

Dega would have seconded him, but Arnau suddenly found it in him to scream out, "Siberia!"

Dega looked at him. "Liar," he said simply.

The flame on his leg reappeared and, as Eric was dousing it, he cried out, "No, no liar! Is Siberia!"

"*Dru, stop!*" At this point, Dega had compassion for Arnau and healed his leg.

"Why did you heal me if you think I am a liar?" Arnau asked, breathless.

Dega looked at him for a very long time and then motioned the others to follow him away from the captives.

Before they could all explode into questions at once, he said, "One question at a time, but first: Dru, never, *ever*, do that again."

"It was effective."

Dega sighed. "We're the good guys here, remember?"

"My point exactly," Dru said, seeming annoyed. "We're the good guys and they're the bad guys, so I still see no problem with it."

Dega shook his head. "More on that later."

Before he could get another word out, Aimee asked, "I have to know, how are you trilingual?"

"I'm not. I used the vocabulary from their minds. The reason I talked so slowly is because I had to find both the words and how to make my tongue pronounce them."

Eric nodded his head, impressed. "Okay, now was Arnau lying or telling the truth?"

"Neither," Dega replied. He tried to think of how to explain what happened. "When he said *Siberia*, I checked to see if it was true. It wasn't, so naturally I called him a liar. But when he insisted that that was where it is, I checked deeper. In his mind I found someone telling him the real location, but what they actually said is dark and mute, so we still don't know. It seems like someone has messed with his mind to delete it and replace it with Siberia."

"How do you know that Siberia was a replacement?" Kandi asked.

"They tried to put it in the same place as the real thing, but what he smelled when he was told Siberia is different from what he smelled when he was really told."

"How could somebody've reprogramed his mind?" Eric wondered.

"Hypnotism, probably," Aimee offered.

"That seems more logical than anything I could come up with, so we'll go with that for now," Dega told them. "And there was something else I found in his mind. It's kind of hard to explain ..." He grabbed a stick and pointed it at the ground. "*This*," he said, pretending to draw a rectangle on the ground, "is a map of Earth. Unless they're really aliens, their base has to be somewhere on this map, yes? Even if it's just a five-thousand square-foot building, it is on this map. Now, Arnau must be pretty important, because they showed him how they attack.

At first it was planned, like we thought, but now it's completely random. They have a ... what's that computer program thing that does stuff for you, Barrett?"

"Do you mean an algorithm?"

"No ... oh well. They have something on their computer that randomly chooses places on Earth to shoot at. Everywhere not under water is on the program, and it chooses off that. The only stipulation is that a place can't be hit more than once until everywhere has been hit."

"That's a scary thought," Kandi said, shivering.

"Yeah," Eric said, "but at least we know something now."

"I'm actually not finished. Listen again. *Everywhere* above water is included. The base has to be above water, so sooner or later, by that thinking, they'll hit themselves. I don't understand it."

Aimee thought for a second. "Get that map that he has in his memory and find every above water place, then put it in your head," she said. Dega looked at her curiously but did as she asked. "Is there any way you could transfer that to my mind?"

"I'm not sure," Dega told her.

He closed his eyes for a second, and then Aimee nodded her head.

"That worked," she told him. She then dropped down to her knees and touched the ground. She was quiet for a very long minute before looking up at Dega and saying, "Look."

"Can you not just tell us?" Dru asked impatiently.

Aimee breathed to steady her composure. "I just got a map of what the *actual* earth is in my head by feeling the ground."

"You can do that?" Barrett asked.

Aimee smiled. "I compared the real version to what Dega got out of Arnau, and there seems to be just a small piece of land missing from what he thinks. It's in the Pacific but not near Oceania. It's out by itself. I can point it out on a map."

CHAPTER 11

"O kay, I think I have it," Dega told the rest of their group after a few hours of debate.

"What?" Kandi asked. Her voice showed how annoyed she was.

"As long as I'm not used as bait again, I'm fine with it," Aimee offered, causing Eric to smile.

Dega proceeded. "After the last missile, the government set up an encampment for anyone displaced that needed stuff like food and water. I think we could use it as a hiding place, at least for a little while. We could mingle with the residents and no one would know us from anyone else. If we're careful, we can stay there while we figure out what to do next."

"What if the terrorists have people doing the same thing?" Dru asked.

"That'll be a chance we'll just have to take. We've just gotta stay together and not bring too much attention to ourselves."

"What about those four guys tied up outside?" Aimee questioned. She could almost see the light bulbs go off in everybody else's eyes.

"I could go kill th—"

"*Dru*," Dega said, cutting her off. "We are *not* going to kill anyone who is not in the process of trying to kill us."

"And what do you think they would do, given the chance? They wouldn't have to think about it. That sounds like they're trying to kill us to me."

"Self-defense, Dru. Right now they're defenseless. That would be slaughter."

"It would be fair." Dru and Dega had both been speaking softer than normal, but power was in their words all the same.

"Fair is not always moral."

Dru was about to respond when Eric jumped in and said, "Let's just hold up a second, y'all." He addressed them both, though his eyes were locked with Dru's. "There are six of us; the democratic thing would be to vote. I think I can speak for Kandi, Barrett, and Aimee when I say we wouldn't stand for murdering them?"

"I'm indifferent," Aimee put in.

"And I don't call it murder, I j—"

"Okay, sorry Dru," Eric said, trying not to rile her up. There was no opposition to his previous statement, less Aimee's half-hearted one, so he then said, "It seems more of us are for not doing whatever it is you call it."

"I have an idea," Kandi started and, when no one stopped her, continued. "What would we do if everything were normal? We would take them to the police."

"You have *got* to be kidding me … " Dru said, annoyed.

"Dru, I know you really don't want to," Eric started, "but, since you see nothing morally wrong with not killing them, could you let us do this?"

Dru thought for what was an uncomfortable second, and then breathed. "Yeah," she said.

"Thank you," Dega said honestly; he thought he saw a slight nod in response.

"So where are we gonna find a cop?" Barrett asked Kandi.

"I think you mean a soldier. There are probably some at the refugee camp," Eric said, starting to laugh. "What?" she asked him.

"Why, hello Private. We have these four men to turn over to your custody; they're part of the terrorist group blowing up the world. Yes, the six of us were able to overpower them, oh, and here are their guns. No, I'm not crazy, why do you ask?"

Everyone was laughing at that point, but Kandi let up enough to say, "We could send one person to get him and have him drive you back here, and then, when you get out, run enough ahead that you could hide and the six of us could leave. The soldier finds the guys tied up when he gets here. We leave a note and hope he believes it."

Dega was still smiling. "That might be the best plan we have. Who's fast?"

"I'll do it," Barrett said, shaking his head.

Kandi had already seen the devastation caused by the missiles in other parts of the country, but now she could put actual live faces to it, faces saddened and scarred. The camp medical tent was so overwhelmed by people that it never closed; the doctors never stopped working.

Dega had told his companions to roam around their large, dirty olive-green tent to talk with the people they shared it with, hopefully gaining information and staying unnoticed. The tent was unfurnished but for the cots lining the wall and the dim lighting; it was the least homely place Dru had ever seen. She,

Kandi, and Aimee walked over to a family of five lying on their cots. They literally had nothing with them but the clothes on their backs.

Dru looked at the parents who acknowledged her, then knelt down to the smallest child, a girl. "Hi," Dru said, smiling. "What's your name?"

When the girl didn't answer—she seemed shy but was also preoccupied staring at the twins in front of her—her mom touched her on the shoulder. "It's okay, Sweetie. Tell her your name."

The girl looked up at Dru but remained silent.

"She's still pretty scared," her dad said kindly.

"I am too, honestly," said his wife. "Josie Hollingsworth."

Introductions were made, and Dru was told her new friend's name was Nancy. As conversation drifted, they learned that the father, Herman, was a teacher at an elementary school nearby. "Did most of the students survive the attack?" Kandi asked him.

Herman's eyes got foggy. "That's where we *weren't* when the missile hit."

As the girls continued their conversation with the Hollingsworths, Eric and Barrett were talking to two brothers at the other end of the tent.

"Hey, how are y'all doin'?" Eric greeted them.

"We're as fine as we can be," one responded wearily. "How about you guys?"

"Same as y'all," Barrett told them. "Barrett," he continued, sticking out his hand.

"Bobby."

"Donny."

"Where're y'all two from?" Eric asked them, trying to seem friendly.

"Boise," Bobby answered.

His brother continued. "We were majoring in computer programming at State then moved here for work." He looked around. "Should have stayed in Boise."

"So how about you guys?" Bobby asked them.

"Gatlinburg, near Knoxville, Tennessee," Barrett answered. He offered no more information than that.

Meanwhile, Dega struck up a conversation with an old man who appeared to have been homeless, even before the attacks.

"How are you today, Sir?" Dega asked respectfully.

"Who's askin'?" the old man retorted.

"Well, Sir," Dega stuttered, taken aback, "my name is Dega. I was just trying to be friendly. A man can't have too many friends at a time like this." The man was silent. "What's your name?"

"Cyrus Mchaelhaney," he answered, with a meanness about him that let Dega know the conversation was over.

"I'm sorry if I bothered you, Mr. Mchaelhaney. I was just trying to make conversation. Have a good night." Dega walked to his bunk.

Barrett looked around their sleeping quarters and—remembering from sight the sleeping people and, aside from that, its bareness—returned his eyes to the conversation and Kandi whispering, "Is there another place near it that we could get to?"

"No, it's literally all by itself," Aimee replied. "That's why they wanted it to be their base."

"At least we know that them comin' from the ocean wasn't just to throw us off," Eric noted. "Maybe they're not bein' too sneaky about other things, too."

Barrett laughed quietly. "Don't bet on it."

"So," Kandi said, continuing her original thought, "if we go, we would have to go to the actual island?"

"Or turn right back around," Aimee answered. "And it's *so* far away from anything else that I don't know about that."

"If you're thinkin' about seasickness, I could make the waves almost nonexistent," Eric offered.

"But could you calm a storm?" Dru asked. "That's what I would be more worried about."

Eric shook his head.

"Wait, so we're actually goin'? Like, now?" Barrett asked, the truth just dawning on him.

"We'll have to sometime; why not now?" Dru said.

Barrett had no response, so he just went with it. "Have we ruled out airplanes?" he asked.

Eric hesitated. "I still don't trust that they wouldn't notice an airplane headed straight for them."

Dega walked in from his information-gathering trip. "Not to mention that we'd be the only plane in the air over the Western Hemisphere. The U.S. has grounded all of ours and convinced the other countries in the Americas to comply."

"They listened to us?" Eric asked, somewhat surprised.

Dega smiled. "None of them wanted to fight the terrorists and the U.S. at the same time."

Eric nodded.

"I can't believe we've been reduced to needing a boat in this century," Kandi said.

"At least one would be easy to get; we'd just need to go to the harbor," Dru put in.

"That was very inconveniently just hit," Dega told her. "About a day sooner and we would've had it."

"Oh well." Aimee sighed. "So what are we going to do about it?"

"There are other places with boats than just docks," Dru said. "There's probably like a boat store or something that hasn't been hit."

"Not bad thinking," Eric said. "When are we gonna go see?"

"I can right now," Dega told him, "but I want to stay here a few days before we leave." He closed his eyes and concentrated on finding locals with helpful knowledge.

"Do you really think so?" Kandi asked over the table in the makeshift mess hall.

"Oh yeah, no doubt." Aimee replied. She glanced past Kandi at a guy two tables back. "He definitely likes you."

"No ... " Kandi said, though she was beginning to smile.

Aimee looked past her again but this time at Barrett as he drew near. "What would your first thought be if I mentioned the guy over there, dark hair, red and black shirt? But don't make it obvious!"

Eric and Barrett both sat down, and Barrett tried to be sly in looking to see who she was talking about. "Oh, you mean the one that's been lookin' at Kandi?"

"No he hasn't been!" Kandi insisted.

"Yes, he has," Dru told her again.

"I disagree!" She seemed a little shy.

"It don't matter none whether you agree or not," Eric said, laughing. "What matters is what's actually happenin'."

Kandi's cheeks were already red; she didn't respond.

Dega sat down and looked at Kandi's face. "What did I miss?"

"They think the guy a few tables behind us likes me. Mr. Talladega? Help?"

Dega laughed. "I'm not going to read his mind, if that's what you're asking." Kandi looked disappointed.

"What's he looking at?" Dru, who was across the table from Kandi, asked.

"Kandi, I assume," Eric said, still smiling.

"No, he's been looking over that way," she motioned, "for the past few minutes."

Just as they looked where she pointed, a man stood from a table with his tray. He added something to the conversation in which he was involved and started laughing before heading toward the trash cans; his path was taking him right behind Kandi, Eric, and Barrett. Dega turned sheet white, but everyone else was so curious that they didn't notice the reason. Kandi's admirer had started walking and met the mystery man about fifteen yards from the group's seats. He put his hand on the man's shoulder, not threateningly but authoritatively; he spoke in the same manner. The other man seemed amused, and Kandi saw him raise his free right hand just slightly and smirk. Kandi's admirer responded, stronger, and the man sliced his right hand at his thigh. He let out a cry, and Kandi realized he had been stabbed. The five Destined, Dega excluded, jumped up, but they weren't quick enough to stop the now-stabbed, infatuated teen from swinging. He was on top of the knifeman fairly quickly, and Kandi was about to go back and sit down, but she noticed three other people moving toward the fight from the other side of the mess hall. Seeing them made it dawn on her why Dega hadn't been quick to move and what was actually going on. She recognized Michael and Arnau, and another quick glance at the bleeding knifeman and she recognized him as one of the four they had captured and tied up the day before.

Eric realized it at the same time as Kandi. It all happened so quickly that he was about five feet away from the fight (and sprinting full speed) when he decided that he would try to end it naturally before using his power. Just as he noticed that the admirer now had the knife and was holding his own quite well, multiple gunshots went off. People started screaming, and then there were two flashes, almost synchronized. Then the flashes were gone, and he could see that two of the terrorists had been burned to death from Dru's fire, and the third, whom he thought was where Arnau had been standing, had been outright obliterated by Barrett. The only one that still had any semblance of a normal appearance had been killed by his own knife.

Dega breathed. He saw that the one who had been flirting with Kandi was lying on the ground bleeding. For everyone else, it seemed time had stopped, but he ran over and healed the teen. Dega could tell he was about to get a question, so he put his hand over his mouth and shook his head. *This would've been a good one for Kandi,* he thought to himself, because he saw a look of acceptance in his face.

Dega stood. Everyone that hadn't already run out was staring at him, Dru, and Barrett. A few soldiers ran in, guns drawn. "Explain, now!" one of them barked.

Dega wasn't in the mood, but he tried to be agreeable. "These four men were working with the terrorists."

"What makes you think that?" The officer seemed unconvinced.

Dega didn't want to give away too much. "We just do. And whether they were or not, they attacked us."

The second officer seemed more scared than anything. "What were those explosions?" He tried to ask his question in a commanding tone.

Dega ignored him and turned to his group. "We need to go."

He started walking toward the exit, and the first policeman positioned his hand to better pull the trigger of his pistol. "We're not done with you."

"Well, *we're* done here." Dega turned his head. "Kandi, if you would."

The guns flew out of their wielders' hands before they knew what was happening and landed at Dega's feet. He gave the two of them a look that said *nope* and headed out, his friends on his heels.

Kandi was in shock that that had actually worked, and to make sure it wasn't a ruse, she turned back to the soldiers right before they went out of sight. They and the refugees were staring in awe. She caught sight of the person who had taken a knife for her; he was looking back. She mouthed a *thank you* and left with her friends.

Not long after they left the camp and hid on a hill overlooking it, they noticed a small band of thirty armed men nearing. They easily overpowered the guards at the main gate, and were thereafter met with little resistance. Dru saw them enter the tent in which she and her friends had slept and looked to Dega, who quietly voiced his opinion that they go after them. There was no objection. They knew that the men had taken the dirt road to the camp from the valley, so they attempted to find a vehicle that they could take down the mountain. By sheer luck, they quickly found the vehicles by which the enemy had arrived.

"Y'all wanna use these, or should I disable 'em?" Barrett asked.

"Let's go ahead and disable them," Dru responded. "That'll confuse them even more than stealing them."

"Wait," Dega said quickly. He pointed to the side of one of the cars, and before long everyone had seen the guard. They quietly decided that killing him would be much too noisy, and so they left him and his cars alone and continued trying to get down the valley unseen. Plans changed a few minutes later, however, when Kandi pointed out that their surroundings gave the perfect opportunity to catch their enemy off guard.

About an hour passed before they heard the trucks' engines, and it was another five minutes before they were close enough for Aimee to open a hole in the ground in the road immediately in front of them. Dru quickly produced her flame inside the hole, burning both men and trucks. Once it was clear that they were all dead, Aimee closed the road back as if nothing had happened.

They began their trek back to their hideout on the hilltop silently when it was finished, all content in their own minds, until Barrett reached to the dirt and picked up something. "What in the world … ?"

He reached it out to Dega, who needed only one look to recognize what he held. "That's a mask that looks exactly like the old man in our tent." As so many times before, he concentrated deeply, seeking the old man's mind. He opened them furrowing his brow. "I can't read anything in his mind. You remember how Arnau's mind had almost been written over in that one place? Mr. Mchaelhaney's is completely that way."

"How did he get away?" Aimee asked, getting somewhat defensive about the possibility that she hadn't managed to kill everyone.

Dega breathed and shook his head. "No idea. He's alone for now, though, so we don't need to worry about him being too much of a threat."

"Too many games," Barrett said. "I don't like it."

"I don't either," Kandi agreed. She paused. "I say we go to their island now."

CHAPTER 12

E ric sat on the deck, just looking and breathing, glad that Dega had been able to piece together enough to find the terrorists' ship. The sky above him was beautifully full of every possible color combination, and under him was the ocean, its magnificence truly emanating. In every direction he saw the two sides meet—the heavens' hues and the sea's grandeur—in perfect harmony. To others on the ship, he knew, the downside came only from the occasional wave that would soak a part of the deck; to him that made it seem more natural. Barrett's voice should have startled him, but he was so calm that it didn't. "Do you feel at home out here?"

Eric considered the question. "Not enough mountains," he replied, grinning.

Barrett heard the slight hint of a question in Eric's quip. "Since you've got water, I figured you were, but I wanted to know."

Eric laughed. "By that logic, you'd be right at home in a thunderstorm."

Barrett smiled. "It sounds horrible, but that's about right."

Eric's amusement was still evident on his face. "Let's see …

Dru would be good in a volcano, Kandi with a tornado, Aimee ... a fault, and ... What about Mr. Dega?"

"A graveyard?" Barrett suggested.

"Anybody that didn't know what we were would think us six are terrible," Eric joked.

"That's about right."

Eric shook his head, still chuckling. For a moment it was serene again, with both admiring the awesomeness of their view. "Red sky at night ... " Eric began the rhyme.

"A good thing, too, because I don't wanna get into any more storms than we have to."

"Wow." Kandi's voice was full of awe. "This is amazing!"

Eric didn't turn away from the open to greet her. "Just like one of those really good pictures, you know, that comes preloaded on a computer."

"About how many more days till we get there?" Barrett asked to anyone who knew.

Dega, Dru, and Aimee stepped out onto the deck in time to hear the question, and Aimee answered. "If we keep going this fast the whole way, it should be about six days, max."

"So that means about five and a half days of plannin'." Eric didn't ask so much as note.

"I don't see how we *can* plan," Dru put in. "We have no idea of what they have and how they have it set up. We don't know how many people are there. We have no information to strategize with."

"You've a point," Barrett said, "but, I mean, there's gotta be somethin' we can do. We've already spent so much time without bein' able to plan or anything."

Kandi looked at Dega. "Is there anything you know that we don't?"

"No, there's really not. We're actually lucky to know as much as we do with how little all our attackers knew."

"Anybody got any cards?" Eric asked.

Kandi laughed. "And just what do you propose we gamble with?" she asked.

"We don't have to gamble; I know a few other games."

"I think there's a deck in the captain's cabin," Aimee offered.

Barrett shook his head, laughed, and followed her off the deck and down into the inner part of the ship. He still couldn't believe that something that seemed so small could hold a room with eight sleeping quarters—the quarters looked like a small convenient apartment, with four sets of bunk beds being the only furnishings, plus the captain's cabin and a small kitchen— but it did. He looked into the open doors as he passed, still trying to make sense of it.

Aimee handed Eric the cards and sat down at the decent-sized circular table.

"Is this really what it's come to?" Barrett asked.

"It's been like this a lot recently," Kandi reminded him. "Do you have any better ideas?"

Barrett sat down.

Kandi jerked her head from her pillow at the thunderclap and immediately felt the waves strongly rocking the boat. It was too dark to see anything outside the captain's cabin where she, Dru, and Aimee were sleeping, and she knew lying back down would probably do nothing more for her than make her sick. So she walked up to the door leading out to the deck—the illumination there was better, but she knew it must have been a bad storm because she still could just barely see—where she found Eric looking out the glass. "Did the storm wake you up too?" she asked him.

He laughed. "It's 7:30 back home; I've gotten back on normal schedule, bein' able to rest the past few days."

Kandi was shocked. "You're usually up this early?"

"If by *usually* you mean *used to be*, then yeah."

"Too early," Kandi said, shaking her head.

"Hey, it's not just me," Eric jokingly defended himself. "If Barrett hadn't stayed up half the night he'd be right here with me."

Kandi again looked outside at the rain. Lightning flashed. "Is there any chance of the boat turning over?" she asked Eric, suddenly a little worried.

"I don't think it will," he told her, "but if it starts to I'm pretty sure I can stop it."

"Could you make the waves stop?"

"No, way too much force and way too many of 'em. But like I said, if we start to capsize, I'll bring some water from the other side to push us back up."

This reassured Kandi, and the two of them sat there in silence until Dru and Aimee walked up. "Is the world ending?" the latter asked with a yawn.

"It sure would make killin' the terrorists a whole lot easier," Eric said, smiling.

"Just a clarification question," Aimee said. "Is that what we're actually doing now? Hoping to kill all the terrorists before we leave their base?"

"Sounds like a plan," Barrett said, walking up behind them.

"Yeah, assuming we can," Dega agreed.

Dru seemed slightly confused. "Why wouldn't we be able to?"

"There are a few of us and a lot of them on their home turf."

"We may be playin' some defense," Eric put in.

"Probably, but we can try," Kandi said optimistically.

"Okay, so answer me this—" Dru said, starting her question.

"How is going in there and killing a bunch of people any more *noble* than killing those four outside L.A.?"

Dega thought how to put his words together before he started explaining. "We had stripped them of their weapons and tied them up; to our knowledge, they were no longer a threat to anyone. Did they deserve to die? Yes. But that was not for us to decide since they weren't putting anyone in danger. These people, they'll all have guns. We'll need to kill them for our own protection. Now, if any of them throw down their weapons and surrender and we feel that we can get them back to the US government without a problem, then that's what we would need to do, the one exception being that we have to kill whoever's in charge. He probably wouldn't give himself up in the first place, but if he did we would still have to kill him because of all the people under him that would do what he said. Does that make sense?"

"You're not honestly considering taking anyone back to the US?" she asked him in disbelief.

Barrett stepped in. "I doubt it'll actually come to that, but if it does we can call it a situational decision." He ended his statement there, hoping that in so doing he had shown enough diplomacy.

"I guess that's fair," Dru told them.

Dega nodded in agreement, and the conversation turned to less pressing things. The sun eventually came out from behind the clouds—the storm was strangely short-lived, considering their location—and Eric went to make sandwiches. He was about halfway through when he heard Barrett's voice. "Hey Eric, come here."

Obediently, Eric left the sandwiches. "Yeah?"

"Listen to what Aimee just realized." Barrett's face looked somber.

Eric turned to Aimee. "During the storm last night, the winds were strong and the waves were high, yes?" Aimee asked.

"Yeah...." Eric said, confused by the obviousness of the remark.

"We're in a boat," Barrett told him.

Eric realized they were telling him that the storm had thrown the boat off course. "So we go to whatever you call a boat GPS and reroute, right? Or can we do that?" The second question was brought about by the fact that they had called him in to tell about it rather than just doing it.

"We could if the boat had a navigation system," Dega explained, "but it's been removed."

Dru shook her head. "It was not the smartest idea on our part to take a boat that had no GPS."

Eric was starting to fully grasp the problem. "So what do we do?"

Aimee answered him. "In a perfect world, we would look at the stars tonight when it gets dark and figure out our position like that, but none of us know how to do that."

Eric half-laughed. "I sure don't." He looked at Dega expectantly but received no answer. "Wait, are we legit lost at sea?"

Barrett was about to affirm when Kandi spoke up. "It may not work, but I've got an idea if you guys are willing to try it."

"Let's hear it," Barrett said, almost gratefully.

"You found the island by searching the earth with your power, right?" she asked Aimee.

"Yeah, but I can't do that now because we're over water."

"We're over water," Kandi said, smiling, "so Eric can do sort of what you did."

"I can't just find one specific island with my only boundary bein' that it's on this planet," he protested.

"Every piece of Earth has a different feel, "Aimee said

thoughtfully. "Could I somehow translate to you what the feel of this island is?"

"No," Dega told her, "but I can."

"I like it," Eric said as he walked out onto the deck. "Have at it, Mr. Talladega."

Dega lowered his head in concentration, and a few seconds later Aimee jerked her head slightly. Eric followed when her *feel* of the island was translated to him, but then turned toward the ocean and concentrated. He looked up at Kandi. "About two days that way," he told her, pointing for a 120-degree change of direction.

Barrett, too, looked at Kandi. "What did you do as a kid to make yourself good at comin' up with stuff like this?"

"I watched basketball, not football," she told him with a sly smile on her face.

"Thou heretic!" Eric joked, following her to help change the course.

"Just two more days..." Aimee said.

"Yeah," Barrett agreed thoughtfully. "I almost wish we'd been blown more off course."

"Think!" Dega cried out. Kandi struggled to make out his silhouette in the darkness; they had gotten close enough to what they had started calling "The Base" that he had them cut the lights. The clouds were gone for the most part, but it was a new moon, and he wouldn't let them use flashlights. Neither rule had been much help, though, when a security light had caught their craft in its beam. They were still a few thousand yards out, so no matter the form of transportation that was sent, they knew they had at least a few minutes. The light had gone out after spotting them for some reason before Dega's exclamation.

"Yellin' won't help anything," Eric said, trying to sound calm.

"It makes me less agitated," Dega replied quickly.

"How in the world did we *not* think of this?" Barrett asked as much as exclaimed.

"To be honest, I did consider it a few days ago," Dega told him, "but since they can't be found by satellites, I just assumed that they wouldn't have anything to find us with."

"How's that assumption working out for you?" Aimee asked sarcastically.

"Shut up and listen!" Dru yelled out. "If you think of an idea, say it. If you don't, keep your mouth shut."

No one was in the mood for an argument, and all complied. "Could we turn and go that way and speed up until we're on the far side of the island?" Barrett asked. "Would that make 'em lose us?"

"They probably have night vision telescopes or something trained on us, I don't think that would work," Kandi put in.

"Night vision telescopes?" Eric asked, somewhat amused. "You never know" was the response he got.

"We could go straight at the island and pretend we're the actual people that are supposed to be on this boat coming back from our assassinations," Aimee suggested.

It was starting to get nervy on the deck. "They probably already know that they're dead," Dega told her. "We would just be quickening our capture."

"Are you sure that would get us captured?" Dru asked. "We can fight."

"I don't want to take the chance."

Kandi spoke up again. "Do you think there's a lifeboat or something that we could get in and then send this boat in another direction?"

"I don't like it," Eric said. "We're in the Pacific. Too many sharks."

"There was a raft in the cabin," Aimee told them.

"In the *cabin*?" Barrett asked. "That's a terrible place for it."

"Yeah, the terrorists must have been really cocky to think that not even the ocean could stand up to them."

"That may be the only plan we come up with." Dega acknowledged. "Will it hold all six of us?"

"Not comfortably, but yes. I'll go get it."

"I'll go angle the boat more northward," Kandi offered. She sprinted off to turn the wheel. When she was satisfied with the change of course, she heard Barrett yelling for Eric to help him carry the cumbersome thing through the not-so-big hallway in the darkness. She came out and lent a third set of hands.

"How are we gonna get it down?" Aimee asked.

Barrett thought for a second. "I remember where some rope and oars are."

"No, I got it," Kandi told him.

"Can you hold us all up in it and let it down gently?" Eric asked, understanding her plan.

She hesitated. "Help me?"

"Of course."

The six of them lifted the raft over the side railing, and Kandi used her wind to hold it up. Then Eric pulled up the water directly under the raft and took a lot of the weight off Kandi. One by one, they got in; Eric and Kandi went last, in case either got too tired. Then they lowered it into the ocean, and the craft they had been in for days went ahead of them. They turned and looked at the base, which could be made out by a few lights here and there. "Let's curve around and hit it from the south," Kandi suggested to Eric.

"As long as we get there without gettin' eaten I don't care where we go."

The gap had closed to less than a mile while they were still in the raft, and after they had covered about a fifth of the remaining distance in the raft, Aimee whispered "Look north."

Kandi did. She saw a boat, lights flashing, speeding from the direction of the island toward where she assumed their boat was—exuberant that, unless it was a ploy, they had managed to escape. She was almost jumping for joy until she saw an orange burst a minute later. "Did they just—?"

Eric was the only one who could find a voice to answer. "If we'd stayed on board for another few minutes we'd have been obliterated."

It took them another thirty minutes to reach the south side of the island, which had proven to be a good choice. Eric ran the raft ashore on a mostly white sandy beach that seemed to completely encircle the island for about two hundred yards before the sand gave way to thick foliage. Most importantly, there were no guards. Dega made the comment that the arrogance of the terrorists was again being displayed, and they probably figured there was no way anyone could ever make it this far. Nevertheless, they decided Eric should sink the raft; Aimee wiped their footsteps from the sand as they searched for a good place to make camp.

CHAPTER 13

The second morning on the island, Barrett woke to the most beautiful sunrise he'd ever seen; the reds, oranges, and yellows that shone over the ocean struck the sand as lightly as the waves and were more magnificent than even those they had seen at sea. And, because of the hiding spot that Eric, Kandi, and Aimee had been able to carve out of the rock wall, Barrett's eyes were shielded from the direct sunlight, enabling him to enjoy the view all the more. He brought his eyes back to his companions and saw Aimee with her back to the wall; she had taken final watch. She felt his eyes on her and looked back at him. Barrett tilted his head toward the view and smiled. She nodded and did the same.

It took another hour and a half before Dru, the last sleeper, woke; they decided that they might not get much sleep anytime soon, and so allowed it. "You missed an awesome view this morning," Barrett said, laughing at the sight of her groggy state.

"Sleep. More important...." She mumbled, trying to wake fully. The day prior had been devoted to rest, but Dru apparently needed more.

"There's a few hundred people on this island," Dega said,

bringing the conversation to the inevitable, "but thankfully they're all on the north side."

"Reason for that?" Kandi asked.

"Not that I can see. Probably just chance."

Eric rose and walked toward the ocean, ignoring the conversation. Keenly aware of his surroundings, he stooped to the water. He expected to sense a few decent-sized fish, but about six hundred yards west he felt a massive object, bigger than any fish that should have been so close to the island. *Beached baby whale,* he thought to himself and started toward their breakfast. He kept track of it and, strangely, found it to be moving toward him. At fifty yards he saw what he had been tracking, turned on his heels, and sprinted toward the group. "Y'all, the boat came up!"

"Do what, now?" Barrett asked, surprised.

"I don't know how, but I guess I didn't sink it well enough," Eric said worriedly. "It's comin' east at a good little clip. I re-sank it, hopefully better this time."

Dega frowned. "Check the top current and the bottom currents of the water." Eric did so and explained them, after which Dega thought for a few seconds before saying, "It probably didn't come up where any person would see it. Too close for me, though."

"Look, I'm sorry—" Eric started.

Aimee interrupted him. "We all make mistakes. This one didn't cause any damage; don't worry about it."

Eric nodded his gratitude. "Now, what were y'all talkin' about?"

Instead of an answer, Dru picked the conversation back up. "Have you figured out what they are?" she asked Aimee.

"Aimee senses some objects protruding out from all over the rock face," Kandi answered the confused look on Eric's face.

"No," Aimee answered Dru. "They're not bombs or mines or anything. But this kills me; I just don't know what they are."

"Can you show us where the closest one is and let us take a look at it?" Barrett asked.

Dega interrupted. "It may be some weapon that's not a bomb; it would be too risky to just walk up to it."

"How else are we gonna figure it out?" Barrett pressed.

"Do we really need to be worryin' about 'em?" Eric asked.

No one responded and the matter was temporarily dropped. Dru asked, "So what now? Do we go around the island and just try to sneak up on them?"

Dega looked at Aimee. "Is there a base or something like that inside this rock, or is it all sitting out on the other side?"

Aimee concentrated. "It seems hollowed out toward the north end, but aside from two doors there, it's solid rock."

"We're gonna have to go around, then," Barrett noted.

"Or," Kandi began, "Aimee can hollow us out a path through the rock."

Aimee started shaking her head. "None of you have ever drained yourself trying to do something with your power, so you may not believe this, but—"

"That happened to me back when we first left Gatlinburg," Eric told her. "We know."

"Around it is," Dru said matter-of-factly.

After eating some fish that Eric caught and Dru cooked, they started around the island. The rock wall soon faded into dense forest, and at first they didn't worry about being quiet, but as they got ever closer they instinctively let silence rule. Fifteen minutes more passed before Eric saw Dega straighten as he walked. He stopped and quietly motioned to the others that they were about to be confronted. They all nodded—Dru actually laughed a little—and stopped in their tracks even before they heard a male voice say "Stop," in a strange-sounding accent.

Having already complied, the Destined simply waited for their attackers to show themselves. A short but muscular man holding a very large gun emerged, leading an obviously-well-trained group of men.

The group encircled their would-be prisoners. "We have orders to take you with us," the leader spoke again. He eyed Kandi and Aimee suspiciously.

Dega managed to get the attention of his comrades fairly easily and gave a quick shake of the head to stop them from attacking yet. They allowed the enemy to lead them into the woods.

Dega went a few hundred feet before speaking. "So has your son's aim improved?"

The troop leader almost tripped over his own feet and, gathering himself, pointed his gun at Dega. "What did you ask me?" His voice was harsh.

Eric had to restrain his laugh when Dega smiled and, in an uplifted voice, responded, "I just asked whether his aim has improved. He's been working on that, right?"

The man swung his gun around, striking Dega in the temple. He fell and reached his hand to his head.

Dru spoke almost immediately. "Can we go ahead and—"

"Shut your mouth, girl!" the troop leader screamed at her. "Did anyone address you?"

Eric and Barrett raised their eyebrows, and Dru glared at the man for a few uncomfortable moments before encircling their captors in fire. They all screamed out in fear, and a few actually tried to run, dying the moment they touched the flame.

"You shouldn't have said a word," Dega said to his enemy after healing himself. He stood, and the opposing commander gave the order to open fire, but in an instant the flame engulfed them, leaving the "captives" alone in the woods.

Eric laughed. "I don't mean to make light of the fact that Dru just killed over twenty people, but that was fairly amusing."

Aimee nodded in agreement.

"We should keep moving," Dega told them, moving back toward the shore. "That was just a random patrol group, meaning they still don't know we're here, but it's possible they saw the smoke from the flame and will send people to see what's going on."

After reaching the edge of the woods, they continued walking until Aimee stopped them and pointed to a spot near the top of the rock—the trees had faded into rock wall again—about forty yards in front of them. Dega guided them all to the base of the wall, hoping to be spared were it something triggered by movement. "Still don't know what it is?" Barrett asked Aimee.

She shook her head. "No idea."

"It's not so much *in* the wall as it is *on* it," Kandi noted.

"Trust me," Aimee defended her earlier statement, "it extends back in there."

"I can knock it down," Kandi offered.

Dega looked at Aimee and, getting no objection, said, "Go for it. But land it gently."

At first the strange object seemed unwilling to budge, but soon started to wiggle. The wiggle turned into a wave-like movement, and it eventually fell, Kandi slowing its descent. The back part of it was silver, but it was black on the part that stayed outside the wall. The only way anyone would be able to see a shimmer from it was if it were still in its place and the sun reflected into their eyes from the camera lens.

For about a second, there was surprise in Barrett's eyes, but then it was gone, and he said, "We really should've figured they'd have these." He walked up behind it and stomped on it a few times before Dru set it aflame.

"I sure feel like an idiot," Eric agreed with him.

Kandi's face showed her worry. "Do you think they've seen us?"

"No." Aimee said, sure of her answer. "This is the first one we've been near."

Kandi was heartened by this until Eric looked at Dega and said, "Where'd the boat come up at?"

Dega responded with a question to Aimee. "Do the cameras extend the same distance from the base to the southwest as they do to the southeast?" She nodded *yes*, and Dega looked back at Eric. "I think it's safe to say they saw it." No one spoke. "We should keep going; we just need to be more careful. Barrett, can you disable those things?" Barrett nodded. "Tell him when you feel us coming up on one, Aimee."

"It wouldn't be suspicious that the cameras are going bad at the same pace someone could walk?" Kandi asked.

"It would," Dega replied, "but at least then they wouldn't know who it is that's here."

They walked along more quickly now that they knew the weapon they had to fight, with Aimee often looking at Barrett and motioning in the direction of a camera; Barrett was quick enough that they didn't have to slow their pace. Screen after screen went black in whatever dreaded room housed the other end of the devices. After a few minutes—though it seemed longer than that to the rapid-beating hearts of the others—Dega whispered, "We're very close."

Barrett was in the process of disabling the third camera they had come to since Dega's warning when Dru heard him yell, "Y'all move *now*!" Dru instinctively did as she was told and sprinted toward a rock that she thought would be big enough for shelter, all the while hoping that the bullets raining down from the machine gunners wouldn't pierce her. As she dove, she heard a faint yelp but couldn't make out whose mouth it came from. She took two quick glances, one to see if her friends were okay, which she couldn't tell, and the second to see what was happening. She saw a large group of men with machine guns at the top of a ledge, and a second, larger group of men armed with long-clip pistols and machetes running toward Dega and the rest of her friends. The second group was too far away to be an immediate threat, and so she set the nearest machine gunner on fire. Amidst the noise she couldn't hear the scream she knew was there, but she did see him collapse. She quickly moved on to a second terrorist and, as she used her fire, noticed that some of the guns on the far end were jamming, and some were twirling back on their masters, unable to withstand the immense wind Kandi had conjured.

Dru looked toward her companions again, hoping this time to be able to see them. Eric, Dega, and Aimee were in the water; Eric had a well-made shield around the three of them using the ocean water, and Kandi and Barrett had found a rock-shelter of their own behind where they had been standing. The terrorists were closing, and Dru could faintly see a crevice in the sand that Aimee had undoubtedly opened. In it, she put her fire, then focused her attention again on the men on the ledge; she didn't want to scare those coming toward their trap to the point that they would stop. A third, then a fourth and fifth fell from their positions. To keep anyone else from using the weapons of the fallen, she set them ablaze, too. Barrett and Kandi seemed to have control of the ledge at this point—though there were some twenty-five to thirty men still firing at them—so she turned her attention to them. Aimee was opening the crevice just enough so they wouldn't see it until they were right on it, and Kandi helped by blowing sand into their eyes. Dru set a large fire behind these men, preventing them from turning back.

Dru hadn't noticed anything happening with water, so she turned to look at Eric. He was still behind his shield of water, concentrating. The seawater around him looked calmer and yet somehow more intimidating than the rest of the ocean; she knew him to be planning something and was about to turn away again when he unleashed his power. The massive vortex of what a meteorologist would call a dangerous wintry mix shot toward the enemy in a fury. They stopped short and started firing their pistols at Eric, though none of the bullets could penetrate the water that was screaming toward them. At the last second, with fear in the eyes of every man, the water suddenly turned away from its path and flew toward Kandi's and Barrett's rock-shelter. It tore through the rock as though tearing through a screen door and the two were only saved by the water slowing and Kandi pushing it back toward the ocean. Before she had a chance to turn and see what Eric was doing, Barrett's lighting strike went toward the men still on the ledge before curving and hitting Dru's rock. She covered herself in heat, and any debris that would have hit her was melted. Now looking at open targets, all the terrorists' guns were firing. Dru had the sense to leave her heat-shield up but felt herself tiring. She could probably go on defending simple bullets for a few days, but Aimee's crevice had closed and the men carrying machetes were closing. And, somehow, her fire had dissipated from behind them. She was about to reset it when she noticed that the machine guns she had melted were once again operational. Before she had time to consider what she saw, she was struck by a machete in the side.

Kandi was able to come out of her shock just in time to have the presence of mind to blow a strong wind to deflect oncoming bullets. She saw all that Dru had seen and couldn't believe it. She tried to use a gust to throw a man near her onto the rocks in the ocean, but he seemed only inconvenienced by her attempt. She motioned to Barrett to disable his gun—Barrett wouldn't have heard her had she spoken—and in frustration the man dropped it and ran. Kandi blew it to Barrett and raised her eyebrows. He shrugged, aimed, pulled the trigger, and saw a man fall.

They were all very close now, and Kandi and Barrett decided it safest to run toward the group in the ocean, but as they were running, Kandi saw the now gun-less man running toward Dru. She tapped Barrett and pointed, but he didn't have time to shoot the man before he slashed at Dru with his machete. Dru crumpled, and Barrett's bullet pierced the assailant's skull. Her wind-shield still protecting them, Kandi led Barrett in a sprint toward Dru, who had been shot three times since being cut. They picked her up and applied pressure to her wounds while running toward Dega, but they were shocked when they noticed what was happening: racing toward them were three Jet Skis—Eric and Dega on one and Aimee on a second. When Eric noticed the members of their group running toward him, he used a wave to push the unmanned Jet Ski to them. Aimee drove up to Kandi who, as soon as she was seated, blew the Jet Ski away from the island to follow Dega. Barrett quickly sat Dru on the third and wrapped his shirt around her side; he applied pressure to her leg with his hands as he turned the Jet Ski on and tried to catch up with Dega so he could heal her.

CHAPTER 14

Dru's color was fading, and her body was cooling much too quickly from the water splashing her; Barrett didn't know how much longer she would last at this rate. He could still feel a pulse, but he wasn't sure whether he felt it weakening. The blood hadn't completely clotted, but the amount of red behind the Jet Ski was considerably less than it had been when he had first set Dru on it. He was fairly certain he was moving too fast for a shark to attack, but for Dru's safety and his own he struck the water around him with electricity, creating larger waves to push them along faster. Dega seemed to know where he was going—either that or he just wanted to go *anywhere* as quickly as possible. It was astounding what had happened during the battle, with Eric's blast attacking him and Kandi and his own bolt shooting toward Dru; Barrett tried not to think about what it could mean.

As Dru's condition noticeably worsened, Barrett saw Dega and Eric slow their Jet Ski as Dega motioned to Kandi and Aimee to keep going. Barrett caught up fairly quickly, and as soon as he was within hearing range, heard, "I am *so* sorry, I got so caught up in what just happened that I didn't even think to check and see if everyone was okay until just now." Dega reached and hovered his hand over Dru's injuries for a few moments. It was fast, though not instantaneous, and Barrett felt Dru's heart strengthen. "Wrap your shirt around her entire body instead of just her leg so she doesn't get too cold," Dega directed. Barrett complied, and they were off, following the now-distant sisters. Dru tried to lift her head and voice something soon after, at which Barrett leaned down and said, "Dega got to you; you're okay now. Try to rest some."

"*Rest?*" Dru asked, dumbfounded.

Barrett shrugged and chuckled.

"Where are we going?"

"Absolutely no idea," Barrett said, again smiling. "I'm just headin' where they're goin'."

Dru shook her head but was quiet until she saw a distant silhouette. "Is that an island?"

"I sure hope so," Barrett replied, "because otherwise that's the most intimidatin' boat I've ever seen in my life."

Dru smiled.

Even before they got off the Jet Ski onto the shore of the obviously-volcanic island, dormant or otherwise, Kandi was already asking her question. "What just *happened*?" She waited for an answer, but Dega was busy disembarking. "I *know* we weren't attacking each other, so what...?" She didn't know how to continue her thoughts.

"Yeah, I didn't mean to send my water into y'all, it just... happened." Eric was distraught. "I tried to bring it back, but it was like it had a mind of its own."

"Is that possible?" Barrett asked.

"Not in anything I've read," Dega told him.

Kandi momentarily left the conversation to ask, "Are you okay, Dru?"

Dru nodded. "And thanks, by the way, Mr. Talladega."

He also nodded. "I'm sorry I didn't notice sooner."

"Back to topic," Eric said, "*What in the world*?"

Dega sighed. "Whether this is valid or not, I don't know, but I'll tell you anyway. You remember the old guy who claimed to be Mr. Mchaelhaney, but we found his disguise?"

"It was a pretty good disguise, too," Aimee put in.

"It was," Dega continued. "I couldn't tell Aimee or Eric during the fight because it would've broken their concentration, but that guy was up on the ledge with a machine gun."

"Are you sure?" Dru asked.

"Very. He had the same memories of our tent at the refugee camp that I did. It could've been no one else."

"What does that prove, except that our terrorists are havin' to double-up on responsibilities?" Barrett asked.

"I noticed he wasn't shooting near the end of the battle, but more importantly, I was curious how he got from the US mainland to here, so I checked his mind." Dega quieted long enough for his comrades to question it. "I found nothing. Absolutely nothing. Even if I'm wrong and this isn't *Mr. Mchaelhaney*, he wasn't born on the island. I see nothing in his memory banks of ever coming here. It was like Arnau's lack of knowledge, except this was stronger and much more complete. I only know of one person that should be able to do that."

"Who?" Kandi asked him.

"Me. And since I'm obviously not a terrorist—I'm not the least bit offended if you're momentarily suspicious—then that shouldn't have been able to happen. I also know only one person who should've been able to deflect Eric's blast and one who could've deflected Barrett's bolt, and those are Eric and Barrett themselves."

The silence let that sink in. "What I'm hearing," Kandi stated carefully, "is that you think that guy in the disguise has the powers of all six of us combined."

Dega shook his head in disbelief. "That's what I'm hearing myself say, too. It makes no sense."

Eric opened his mouth to speak a few moments before he actually did, giving his words time to form themselves. "I felt really good when we were in the camp and I felt really good when we were on that last island. Until now I thought the reasons were that I was around a lot of people and because I love the ocean and the space. I just realized that I hate bein' around a bunch of people that I don't know and I hate all this scenery that doesn't include mostly mountains."

Kandi had the bravery to voice what everyone else was thinking. "There's a seventh."

"That's gotta be it," Barrett said. He looked at Dega. "Did you not research this?"

"I did, bu—"

"Intensively?"

"Yes. There was absolutely no mention of seven. It was always six."

"All down through ancient cultures, seven was the number of either luck or perfection," Barrett said. "Is there any way someone could've deleted it from history?"

"I'm gonna be completely honest with you: I don't know anymore. Instinct is *no*, but I really don't know."

"It's the only thing that makes sense," Aimee said.

"Real quick," Kandi started, "how long would you say before all the people with guns get here?"

Dega smiled for the first time since getting to this second

island. "I wouldn't have let us talk so long if they were coming. It's possible I wouldn't notice the *seventh*, if he exists, but there is no one else coming."

"How about on the island?" Eric asked.

Dega concentrated for a moment and then got a strange look on his face. "There are three people literally inside the island."

Aimee's interest was piqued. "How is that?"

"Might as well find out," Barrett said.

The nearest entrance into the island's mountainside was dark and dank. Dru had convinced herself that it couldn't possibly have been a passageway used by the terrorists, but eventually they started seeing light bulbs which, inconveniently, were off. Barrett lit every last bulb in the tunnel in the hopes that the people would think it was some kind of reverse-short in the system. Everyone tried to be calm, but no one could; they were walking into the middle of a volcano. Aimee assured them that they weren't actually *in* the volcano, as she couldn't feel the mantel of the earth. Words from her mouth were of little comfort to even herself, though, and they kept walking in fear and without assurance. The tunnel suddenly turned, and it seemed they were headed straight toward the center of the mountain. Still, though, Aimee insisted they couldn't be connected to the actual volcano.

"What's that smell?" Barrett asked after a few more minutes.

"Probably volcanic something," Kandi replied.

Dega whispered, "No, I've been to Hawaii, and that is definitely not a volcano smell. It smells odd; I've never smelled anything like it before."

His whispers made the rest understand how close to the

aforementioned three people they actually were, and they quieted. It only took another minute and a few curves before they were on a ledge in the middle of a very large, open room. The ledge was wide and extended all around the wall, and there were sets of stairs leading up and down at quarter-intervals; Barrett estimated they were on about the fourth story out of ten, with the top four being much farther apart than the rest. The ground/floor was too far down to see in the dim light.

"Not a volcano?" Dru asked Aimee, who held her hands out to say she didn't understand.

"Where are they?" Barrett whispered quietly to Dega, who responded by pointing across the gulf and downward. Barrett looked but saw no one.

"Aside from this opening, there are three doors disguised in the wall," Aimee whispered. "One where he pointed, one a story up and directly above us, and one on this story directly across." She looked at Dega worriedly.

"I assure you there are only three terrorists here, and they're all where I pointed."

"Should we go down there or see if we can take care of them from here?" Kandi asked.

"I vote for as little walking as possible." Dru put in.

"Sorry, Dru," Dega told her, "but I need to be close." They walked around the ledge carefully, with Aimee in the lead to make sure there were no false steps. They began a nearly vertical descent to the door and reached it quickly. "Don't kill them."

"Are you being serious?" Dru asked him.

Dega ignored the question and turned to Aimee. "Could you open the door?"

"No," Aimee responded.

Dega looked at her strangely. "It's just ground."

"They made it look like that," Aimee told him, "but it's really metal. I can't do anything to it."

"And it's heat resistant," Dru offered. "I can tell."

"Well what *can* we do to it?" Eric asked. "Rusting metal would take way too long."

"Could we try and force it open?" Kandi suggested.

Barrett shook his head. "It's electrified. I think I can short it...." He put his hand to where he thought the crack of the door was. For a few seconds he didn't move, and then he seemed to slump back from it as the lights dimmed and came back to full power.

"You good?" Eric asked him worriedly.

"Yeah," Barrett replied, taking a breath. "Just tired. There's a ridiculous amount of backup power. No way to short it."

Punctuating his sentence was the sound of dozens of guns firing at once. Dru immediately produced a shield of fire inside of Eric's ice to try to stop the bullets from reaching them. Occasionally one would get through, but the majority were stopped.

"Melt the guns!" Dega yelled at Dru over the noise.

"In a *volcano*?" she yelled back, amazed.

"Do it!"

Dru got up from her crouch and tried to see where the gunmen were, but couldn't. It seemed like the shots were coming from everywhere, but she saw no one. Sensing her trouble, Barrett got her attention and patted the wall behind them. Dru's eyes lit up, and she dropped her shield—more bullets now made it through, but it was a chance that had to be taken. Against the entire wall for two stories in both directions she placed a short burst of flame, which she almost immediately removed except at the points where she felt something burning. Eventually all the shooting stopped, and Barrett said, "I cou—"

"You've done better than I thought you would, being only

six." They all jumped and turned toward the middle of the cavern where stood a man in his forties with broad shoulders, deep-set brown eyes, and dark hair. Only he wasn't standing so much as floating, and they all knew him to be a hologram. He continued, "But seven less six be cardinally first, and be, yes, in all, no?"

Dega looked into the eyes of the hologram as it faded away and quietly responded, "Neither in heart nor the like." Then two guns went off from behind them, and Barrett and Eric slumped to the ground as Dru incinerated the guns of the men standing in the now open doorway, and Kandi blew each man hard against the wall as the third man raised his hands and yelled, "I give up!"

Dega quickly healed Eric and Barrett and then gave Dru a look that pacified the fire on her hands. He then turned to the man with his hands raised.

"I swear I'm not one of them!" the young scientist said nervously.

One of the other scientists, still held firmly against the wall, snarled something in a clipped tongue. Eric looked questioningly at Dega, who was shaking his head and smiling. Sensing the question, Dega looked at him and said, "He said *be quiet, you imbecile!*"

Dega turned back to their three captives but was blocked from gathering too much from their minds. It was obvious, however, that the scientist still standing before him, a handsome, black-haired man in his late twenties named Peter, was telling the truth. He looked at Aimee. "Bind those two with rock or something. Peter and I are going to have a little talk."

"I'll come," Dru said as she started walking toward him.

"I'd rather you didn't," Dega responded softly. "It would be an extra mental presence for me to have to deal with." Dru seemed disappointed but complied.

Dega motioned for Peter to follow and led him up the stairs to the ledge above. He then turned and looked at Peter for what Peter felt to be an uncomfortable while, though he allowed it in silence. Then Dega spoke. "Okay Peter, so you say you're not like the other two? Then who are you, why are you here, and why should I believe you?"

Peter showed some surprise at the use of his name, but then ignored it. "You probably shouldn't believe me, but you have to. I didn't know what I was getting into when I applied for this job. All I knew was that the pay was three times better than what my college-friends were getting paid with their diplomas; I thought I was applying for a job that worked on medical and nutritional research. I'd been working at my first lab for about three months when they pulled me aside and asked if I'd like to advance in the company. They said they'd been pleased with my work in the lab and wanted someone like me to help them 'make the world a better place.'" Peter paused momentarily. "Of course, who would say no? I accepted, and they told me that my new lab would be in the tropics and that I'd love the scenery. Another ridiculous lie. After they got me here they told me to either work on the weapons with the other scientists and live or protest about being here and die. I chose to live."

Dega began feeling sympathy for the man but tried not to let his emotions get too strong too quickly. "So what do you know about the weapons program? Or anything else that they've got going on to try to kill us?"

"It's not just you; they would've done that to anyone that came looking around the island. They're really looking for the Destined."

"That's what I meant when I said *us*."

Peter's face showed surprise and awe. "To answer your question, you are the people our leader is trying to kill. We were working on weapons that could strike from a distance so our soldiers wouldn't have to be in the range of your powers. And some that could neutralize your powers if you ever attacked us. Some of these weapons are in their infant stages, but a few of them are close to done."

"Do you have access to information we can look at?" Dega asked him, sensing how close they'd come to being too late.

"Yeah, yeah," he said quickly. "It's all in the lab."

"Good, let's go," Dega said, wasting no time.

When they got back to the others, Barrett turned to them and said, "Y'all have a nice talk and get everything figured out?"

"Not everything, but we know more than we did ten minutes ago. Two of you need to guard them," Dega motioned toward the wall, "and everybody else is coming with us."

"I'll stay," Dru told him.

"I will, too," Eric offered. Neither he nor Dru had forgotten his and Barrett's wounds.

Dega turned toward the two captives. "You two need to remember what happened a few minutes ago. I strongly suggest you don't tick them off."

The scientists remained silent but did as they were told, realizing they were no longer in charge. They also realized that it was Dru who had melted their guns and burned their hands.

The rest of the company walked up two sets of stairs in the main room of the volcano and began walking around the ledge. "What was with that hologram?" Kandi asked when it was obvious conversation had ceased.

Dega turned to look at her. "He essentially said that he was the seventh power, and that he was greatest without us. I told him that our hearts were greater than his."

They stopped when they had walked to the far side of the tunnel. Peter pulled a card out of his pocket and touched it to the wall, which opened for them. Dega immediately began the questions. "The missiles that were shot all over the world: Where did they come from and what exactly were they?"

"They were a new type of missile we made that has the same power as a normal nuke but doesn't leave radiation," Peter answered. "I won't bore you with the details," said Peter.

"That explains why we didn't get any radiation when we were at the explosion sites," Dega said thoughtfully.

"You've been to some of the places we hit?" Peter asked in amazement. Dega nodded. "What were they like?"

"Well, your missile worked just fine," Dega told him, not enjoying the tone in Peter's voice.

Peter's look changed to horror. "They told me that they were only for defense..."

"They may've told you that, but it was obviously a lie. Where are the missiles kept?" Dega asked him.

"Here." Peter motioned back toward the center room. To the questioning look on Dega's face, he continued, "This isn't a real volcano; the leader made it out of the ocean floor. He just made it look like a volcano so it wouldn't be suspicious. The floor in the main room opens; that's where they are." Peter again was quiet. "Where have they hit?"

"Cities of every size in every country," Dega told him. "Some of the smaller towns were wiped out completely. It made it worse that we couldn't detect them on radar."

A light seemed to go off behind Peter's eyes. "Now it makes sense. The engineers building the missiles had to put some sort of rock on them. They called it *razim tsapeskileoa tee-ep*, which means something like *unseen bird*. The entire island is made of it; it must been kind of an anti-detector thing." Dega saw a look of resolve in Peter's eyes. "I can't change what has already happened," he said, "but I can help you stop what hasn't."

"I'm glad to hear it. Start by telling us what's planned and what else you're working on."

"Probably the most important thing to mention would be our special uniforms. When you're wearing them, you're invisible."

"Whoa!" Barrett exclaimed.

"That explains how we were discovered so many times in Los Angles," said Dega. "They were probably near us the whole time.

"Would you not have sensed them?" Aimee asked.

"No, I wasn't trying." Dega turned back to Peter. "What else?"

"Our leader said that if you were apart from each other you'd be vulnerable, so we've been working on some stuff for that. Basically he just wants control of the world and seems to think he needs all of you dead to have it." Again Peter paused. "I hope you guys know that I only chose to help because I panicked when they threatened me. And I never really thought about how serious this was."

Peter's voice barely wavered, but Eric could tell that, in his own analytical-scientist way, Peter was actually sorry. "Listen," Dega told him reassuringly, "don't worry about that. If you help us take down your leader, then we'll get you back home."

CHAPTER 15

"They're coming," Peter said upon returning to them.

They looked at him, not questioning what he meant; they knew well enough. Forces were being gathered and were beginning the short journey to the island. Soon there would be battle and, if Dega was right, more would be killed by the Destined at one time than had been killed total. Barrett didn't like it. He looked up and got a worried expression on his face. "It's gettin' to be dark. You don't think they'd attack after nightfall, do you?"

Dega looked at him. "If they do, we have the advantage in that we don't really need light. And we're almost ready." Dega looked up and scanned the island; he was standing with his friends on a rock that rose above the coast just inland of the shoreline. He looked in the general directions of each of the traps that they'd prepared and sighed.

Not knowing him well, Peter interrupted his thoughts. "Where should I be when the battle starts?"

Dega looked at the man and noticed for the first time that he couldn't be older than thirty. This was one who hadn't chosen to come here on his own, as had the other scientists—whom Dega had placed, bound, on the shore to meet their leader—nor had he been chosen by the powers; he had been put into this situation simply by the power of evil. "You should be wherever you want. You have absolutely no obligation to fight with us; helping us prep pays your debt to humanity, at least in my eyes. You're completely free."

Peter stopped short when he realized the meaning of Dega's words but then made his decision. "I want to be where I can be the most help to you guys."

Dega nodded. "In that case go get a gun and stay with me in case I need a messenger." He turned and faced everyone else. Here he stood with two of his former students, two farm kids, and a runaway, all about to face their fates at his side. Before them would be a massive host with the mission to kill each of them. He couldn't offer to switch places with them, as it was also his fate, and he couldn't offer to them the option not to continue, as it was not his to offer. Each of them had been chosen and would have to see it through. "Do you guys know what you're supposed to do?" Dega asked them.

Five nods affirmed. Kandi spoke up. "I'm not gonna give a speech, but I want all of you to know that I really care for you and hope we get out of this okay."

"Same here," Eric said. Everyone was again in silent agreement, waiting.

After a few hours had passed, Dega looked away from the branch he had been toying with and toward the ocean. A few seconds later Eric followed suit. When the ships were close enough for the lights to be seen, Aimee asked, "Are you sure they won't attack until morning?"

"No," Dega answered her simply.

"I've got a feelin' we all should get into position," Eric told them.

"Okay," Dega agreed. "Put on your invisibility clothes and go. If we decide to strike first, I'll have Peter run down to Barrett to disable whatever they use to communicate between boats and to shoot lightning at one of them."

Before they separated they heard four gunshots. Dega noticed Dru's hand burning brightly. "Dru, stop!" The flame dimmed. "They just shot the other two scientists."

"Why?" Kandi's voice asked.

Aimee answered. "They didn't know whether they'd defected to us."

It was a few hours after midnight but still some time before dawn, when Dega made his decision. Before speaking he looked again at the scores of ships just off the strand, their beams clearly visible in the new moon. "Go tell Barrett to shoot, and then come back."

Peter ran as quickly as possible—his knowledge of the island aided his speed, and the invisibility materials that the Destined had allowed him to wear kept him from being confined to the shadows. It took him nearly ten minutes of sprinting, but eventually he reached Barrett and Kandi. "Dega says now," he panted.

Barrett yelled and almost punched at the empty space that had just spoken to him before remembering what was going on. When he did, he looked toward the coast. "Tell Mr. Talladega that communications are cut, at least as far as I can tell. How long do you need before I attack?"

"Fifteen minutes would be nice," Peter told him as he turned to leave, still breathing heavily.

When it seemed the fifteen minutes were up, Barrett said, "We win or die."

"Agreed," Kandi responded.

A great flash cut through the dark night, connecting for a split second the two forces. It looked to hit a ship, but no fire or explosion followed. The energy seemed to converge on itself at an invisible boundary; a ball of yellow glowed hotly. Without warning it sprang back at them. Barrett tried to control it but wasn't strong enough; he knew he was about to die. But then it seemed to falter from its path and fell to the sand about five yards in front of them, like the effect gravity has on a ball that's not thrown quite strong enough. He stared in amazement.

"I remembered what happened at the last battle," Kandi told him. "I got the plan to take all the air molecules out of the space in its path, leaving the ground as its only option."

"Science," Barrett said, almost laughing. "I like it."

To their west, a glow was seen in the darkness. It started out dim, but as time passed it grew hot and bright, bright enough that Barrett could see one ship of soldiers disembarking into rowboats to paddle to shore. Eventually others followed, and before long every ship had lost its army to the water. They reached the shoreline, seemingly waiting for direction. All was still and quiet for a few uncomfortable minutes. Then Kandi heard a gunshot come out from where the fire was, and the foremost soldier fell. A few moments of shock for the soldiers passed before they realized what had happened and fired toward the flame. Kandi assumed Dru had a fire shield to protect them.

With communications down and seemingly no one in command, a number of the troops of their own accord separated themselves from the rest of the host to march toward the fire. The remainder watched apprehensively.

They neared the flame and began to look for the cause. As they searched, they tried to be as silent and invisible—the latter made Eric laugh—as possible, but even so they could see almost nothing in the darkness beneath the trees. A noise seemed to be coming from the ocean, and most barely had time to look before the tsunami-like wave crashed down and dragged them out to sea, drowning them.

Even at his distance from the enemy and with the poor lighting, Barrett was able to see how confused they were. Then he felt a tap on the arm that he knew to be Kandi's reminder. He got the message and grabbed a tree just as the island was beginning to shake; if he hadn't known better he would've looked toward the volcano peak for the coming eruption. The movement of the earth extended out a distance under the waves, which were steadily growing. The ships began rocking to and fro, rising with the waves before plummeting downward; for most it was havoc, and (with Eric's assistance) more than a few capsized.

The roar of the island scared the troops into a retreat back to the shoreline, but the Destined combined their powers into a great storm, causing the elements to send forth a fury, trapping the soldiers on shore. The sheer ferocity of the storm made the soldiers seek refuge in the forest, splitting them into smaller groups. They were still confused and scared as they attempted to weave their way through the trees, the ground still shaking beneath them.

The Destined began to confront the troops, aided by their invisible clothing. Dru would melt the weapons of as many as she could; the ones she didn't get to in time were electrocuted or had the bullets fired from their guns turned back upon them.

When they had almost finished ridding the island of their enemy, they came across a large group of troops; dispatching them took enough time that a few of the troops were able to fire a few rounds from their weapons, striking Barrett and Eric. The tear in their clothing disabled whatever science had kept them unseen, so that they were completely visible. They could still fight but just had to stay behind cover.

The battle for the island lasted into the morning and early afternoon, with most of the enemy's troops fighting bravely in a war they could not win. The few that realized fighting meant death decided that their only chance to survive was to swim back to the main ship, but the waves were too much for them and they drowned.

Victory was finally achieved. No troops were left alive on the island, and only a few were still alive on the twelve ships still afloat. Dega had Barrett bring back communications to the ships and picked up a radio off the body of a dead officer. "Dega to Command," he said simply.

"This is Command, who is communicating?" asked the radio operator.

"The guy behind you knows. I suggest you give him the microphone."

There was silence for a few seconds and then a new voice. "Good afternoon, Mr. Talladega. So nice to finally speak with you. Did you enjoy my party last night?"

"I would hate to see the real party." Dega kept his voice calm. "I've got a question for you: were the lives of so many men worth trying to prove a point? Are you so heartless to continue this war, even after seeing the slaughter last night?"

"I will *not* relent!" He screamed, though he regained his composure before speaking again. "I strive toward an attainable and desirable goal."

"If that's how you want it, but remember us and the entire reason for our existence. You know the histories, I'm assuming. We know them now, too."

A sigh came out of Dega's radio. "It's amazing that you don't understand how much greater my power is than yours."

"Only if you separate us, and I don't see that happening."

"Dega, you are a wise man, but I'm wiser because I don't need other powers like you do. Until we meet again, but I'll see you long before you poor souls see me." His voice ended firmly.

"*Et bon voyage* to you, too."

Not wanting to dwell on the conversation in front of the others, Dega quickly changed the topic by saying that the ones they had killed would be given a decent burial.

"Are you bein' serious?" Eric asked him, amazed. "They tried to kill us! I'd be good with just throwin' 'em all to the sharks."

"They were fighting for what they believed in," Dega said firmly. "We're better than them in that we care about all humanity. Right?"

The burial didn't take long. Aimee opened a large hole in the ground, and everyone else used their powers in various ways to get the bodies into it. Seeing what they had done the previous night was sobering, and Dega, Eric, and Aimee needed to go for a walk alone to think and pray.

When they had all drifted back together, Dega broke the silence. "I know this has been a very physically draining day; the enemy absolutely put us through it. We won, but now he's probably more willing to use the full extent of his power against us."

"That's saddening," Dru said emotionlessly.

Dega turned to Peter. "Is there somewhere we could stay tonight that's hidden?"

"I think I could find somewhere."

"Good, we all need to get a good night's sleep, and I vote it starts right now."

Dru perked up. "I'll second that," she offered.

CHAPTER 16

hile the Destined rested, Peter went through all the research from his laboratory trying to find something he had forgotten about that they would find beneficial. He didn't have any luck for a few hours, but after a few minutes of going through the work of his fellow scientists he discovered that they had been working on something about which he hadn't been informed. Curious and somewhat fearful of the possible implications, he worked through the night, trying to figure out what the equations and seemingly meaningless lines of variables meant.

Around sunrise, Peter realized that he had uncovered what his comrades had been working on. He knew Dega was tired but thought his discovery was too important to wait and so went to wake him.

Dega squinted when he opened his eyes. Peter shushed him and led him a few yards away from the rest of the group. "Last night I figured it couldn't hurt for me to go through the lab, you know, see if I'd forgotten about something…"

"Yeah?" Dega said groggily. "Find anything?"

"You could say that," Peter replied. "The other two had been hiding something from me. Apparently this island has more strange minerals than just *unseen bird*. I don't know why it has so many; probably they were on the ocean floor and that's why he chose to raise the island here, but anyway, the island itself is essentially a bomb. If the minerals and rocks are mixed right, it basically creates a weapon of mass destruction."

By this time Dega had become alert. "Are you serious?" Peter nodded. "We need to get off this island and destroy it."

"That's what I was thinking," Peter agreed. "I'm not sure if I mentioned this, but there's a dock under the island. I'm sure there's a mini-sub there we can take."

Dega went to wake the others. It took some convincing and some shaking, but eventually everyone was awake enough to at least have a conversation. Peter explained to them what he had told Dega.

"So what's the plan?" Eric asked—he was easily the most alert.

"First of all, we're getting off the island," Dega answered.

"Yeah," Barrett said, "yeah, I kinda got that part."

"My vote is to make a bomb from the minerals to actually destroy the island," Peter put in.

"That's reasonable," Aimee agreed. "Can you build it?"

"Yes," Peter assured her, "I spent so much time with this last night that I'm positive of it."

With that they began the trek behind Peter down into the depths of the island. It didn't take long to find the dock. "Why did they leave a sub here?" Kandi asked upon seeing the small craft.

"Probably in case the seventh needed to leave without anyone noticing," Dega told her.

Dru suggested that it might be booby-trapped, but between Peter and Barrett they determined that it was perfectly safe.

Barrett went straight to the weapons control center as soon as he entered the sub. "Could we just fire at the island since it's a bomb in itself?"

"We could try," Peter told him. "It might not work though, and I'm not in the mood for taking the chance. It really would be better if I made a bomb and we shot a missile at that."

"Wait," Kandi said cautiously, "you said it would be a *weapon of mass destruction*. How would we be safe?"

"If we fire from a few thousand yards away we'll be fine."

"Are you sure?" Eric asked.

"Very."

"So are we all good with this?" Dega asked.

No one objected, and Peter took Aimee to help him find the necessary minerals to make the bomb while everyone else acquainted themselves with the sub.

A few hours passed before Peter and Aimee returned. "Where are we gonna put the bomb?" Eric asked Peter.

"There are two options," Peter answered. "We could put it at the base of the mountain and use GPS to shoot a missile, or we could put it in here and shoot a torpedo."

"They'd be able to see where the missile came from," Dega put in. "I'd feel more comfortable with the torpedo."

No one dissented. "So," Peter said, holding out an odd looking structure, "I'll just set this on the dock here—" he did so "—and we can be on our merry way."

They all climbed back into the sub carefully, wary of even the slightest possibility of disturbing the weapon that lay so near to them. Dega took the controls and maneuvered the sub—very slowly at first—down into the water and away from the dock.

"This isn't anything like the speed boats I drove around in Miami all the time," he said, trying to lighten the mood. No one responded, though, and so he let the matter drop.

The sub entered a tunnel that Dega knew led to the ocean. He took it slowly at first, not wanting to strike the tunnel walls and damage the sub, but when he exited the tunnel he pushed the controls to full speed and asked Eric to make the water push them faster. A few minutes later, Peter told Dega they were far enough away from the island to fire. Dega turned the craft around to face the direction from which they'd come and fired. They looked out the periscope and waited.

It didn't take long. The torpedo struck much faster than expected with a large blast that stunned the entire group. All of them but Dru shielded their eyes from the explosion; Dru's fire let her look at it. Then all but Eric braced themselves for the extremely large waves coming toward them; Eric was too busy bracing their craft.

Silence followed, and Dega took their submarine back under the water. "Is it over?" Dru asked.

"No," Dega told her simply. "That took the resources for their weapons, but their commander still has his powers. We're not through."

"What's his name?" Eric wanted to know. "We've been fightin' this guy for a good while now and we still don't know, do we?"

Dega looked at Eric. "I've not told you because I believe he gave up his existence and everything that went with it—including his name—when he allowed himself to be subjected to the seventh power. But if you really want to know, his name is Riker."

"That's not as scary as I thought it would be," Dru said.

"When parents give their kids names," Barrett explained, "they don't know yet what type of person the kid'll grow up to be."

Dru nodded. "So if it's not over, where are we going?"

Eric answered before Dega. "To end it. We're headin' to that first island to finish them."

Kandi started to say something, but her eyes got big and her thought process visibly changed. "*Riker,*" she said, almost spitting the name out, "didn't really use his powers yesterday, did he?"

"I noticed that too," Aimee told her. "Were we wrong to think he had all the powers?"

"We weren't," Dega told them, "and he didn't. I'm not entirely sure why, but I have a feeling he won't hesitate this time. Either he dies or we do."

The Destined let that sink in, but Peter seemed confident when he said, "I'm almost certain we're not going to be the ones that die. The bomb that we just exploded a second ago, I brought three more with us. The other island is larger, though, yes? That's what I thought. We could put them around the island to completely destroy it."

"*You brought bombs onto the sub?*" Kandi asked in disbelief.

"I didn't tell you because I knew you would worry. Look, the sub just endured a big explosion, and we're still here. It'll be okay."

"Would blowing up bombs on the island not end up killing us, too?" Kandi asked him.

"If we get desperate, yes, but we would know; it would be a conscious decision to kill ourselves in the process. It wouldn't be as hard as you'd think to set them off without being near them."

"Where do you suggest we put them?" Dega asked him.

"I don't know; I've never been there before."

"Seriously?" Eric said, mistrusting him slightly.

"They wanted me working on weapons. If you hadn't figured it out, they don't give much vacation time."

"Fair enough."

"How long until we get there?" Peter asked, turning to Dega.

"Not very. A few more minutes, I'd say."

"Are we gonna try to show up unannounced or go in guns blazin'?" Barrett asked.

"We can go in without setting off any alarms," Dega stated, "and we should, but it won't be unannounced. *He* will know."

CHAPTER 17

The night had settled in around them, and what little light had been available during the daytime had dissipated. During a very heated discussion earlier, someone—Eric had forgotten who—calmed the rest by suggesting a compromise of the ideas: they would approach the island from the side opposite the one they naturally would come to first and wait for darkness to attack. The anticipation could be only detrimental to their fighting abilities, Eric had thought, but anything to make everybody else quit yelling. He began to look at the faces of his companions but stopped as he realized the light would bend around their suits and he wouldn't be able to see them. The fabric had been another reason not to wait for night—darkness would be rendered moot—but now it didn't matter.

Dega took a long, deep breath and cleared his mind. It was time. "Roosevelt said that we have nothing to fear but fear itself. We need to remember that. And let's remember why we're fighting: Not for us or for revenge but to make the world a safer place for everyone else. We are Destined because we're supposed to be the source of people's hope. We've kept a low profile, but we're still where that hope lies, whether people know or not. Let's act like it and finish this tonight." Immediately there came into his mind thoughts of his compatriots who he felt duty-bound to protect; they had trusted him, but he wasn't sure he could deliver.

Dru's voice dispelled his thoughts. "Let's do this."

Everyone was silent after Dru's words, each person going back into the comforts of the mind, back to the beach, back to the mountains, back to home. None of them were really emotionally ready, but they had to be. So they were. They did, however, know their jobs—Peter, Eric, and Barrett were to plant the bombs on the island; everyone else was to try to make the job somewhat safer for the three of them. They still knew that Riker was there, waiting for them to make the first move, thinking that no matter what piece was moved against him, he'd still get a checkmate in just one more move. They knew that speed was essential to prevent him from having time to think, that all they needed to do was succeed in knocking the board off the table and it would be over.

The sub's hatch opened, and Eric heard Dega's foot hit a higher rung on the ladder. Just then a gun went off, and something fell to the floor.

"I'm okay," Dega said quickly. "Am I visible?"

"No," Kandi answered, her voice somewhat shaken. More guns fired at the opening.

"Good, then I wasn't hit. It looks like we'll have to start from here."

The land in the general direction of the shooters burst into flames, and Eric knew that in a few seconds they would be able to safely get out. But just as quickly as the flames appeared, they were gone, and Dru gave a small sigh. "It's like my power was drained for a second," she said.

"That means Riker's here, then," Eric said nonchalantly.

For a few moments no one spoke—it wasn't necessary, for they all instinctively knew how to proceed. The land was engulfed in flames again, and then a windstorm and lightning strike came simultaneously toward the men and a tidal wave from the side. The earth shaking beneath them was the real attack, though; not a soldier was left standing. Not all had died, Dega knew, but they had either fallen or run.

The flame had quickly been quenched by an unseen force, but with Riker's effort spent on that, there wasn't enough time for him to stop everything else. The earthquake wasn't as strong as Aimee would have liked, and Barrett's strike didn't hit quite where he had aimed, so they assumed those were what Riker considered the biggest threats.

But the important thing was that it worked. One by one, they all climbed from the craft and into the water. Occasionally a shot would ring out, but none were hit.

Save Eric, who had arrived much earlier, everyone reached the shore at about the same time. Eric quickly removed the seawater from their clothes and bodies, and they set off. Kandi and Aimee went searching for troops, while Eric, Barrett, and Peter went to plant bombs. All of them were trying to get out alive.

Once they were away from the place where they had come ashore, Eric asked Peter and Barrett, "How are we supposed to be able to know where we all are if we can't see each other?"

"There won't be a visible way," Peter answered.

"Good job, thanks," Barrett told him sarcastically. "Could we use our voices?"

Again, Peter answered. "We should probably try not to make a sound when we get into the trees. We don't know where all the terrorists are."

"I'm not about to be tied to y'all or anything," Eric said.

"Well I can't think of anything else," Barrett told him.

"The simplest thing to do might be to determine the location we're going to and just meet up there," Peter suggested.

"If we have to, we have to," Eric told him. "Where're we headin'?"

"I basically cut the island into thirds on a map," Peter explained. "We're putting a bomb at landmarks near the middles of each third. The closest one is a rock about nine or ten yards tall that's shaped like a duck."

"Are you being serious?" Eric asked, chuckling at the thought of it.

"Yes, I know it's amusing, but it's distinguishable."

"Which way?" Barrett asked him.

"Face the moon. Now turn thirty degrees counterclockwise—"

"You're gonna have to explain better than that," Barrett said, cutting him off.

"Turn about one-twelfth of a circle to your left. Go straight and you can't miss it."

"When do we know we've gone too far?" Eric asked.

"When the incline to the center of the island becomes steep, then you've obviously passed it."

Instinctively they understood that it was time to be silent and begin the journey. As they walked into the growth, they heard a few muffled gunshots in the distance; they were soft enough that in any other situation one might not have known what the sound was. Here, they knew. No one stopped, though, as they knew that the longer it took Peter to place the bombs, the longer their friends were in danger of being killed.

They walked for a very long time uninterrupted—almost to the other side of the island—their paths unperturbed by the enemy. It was so seemingly peaceful and the night air so warm that Eric felt almost happy. Reality set back in, though, when his ears were filled with the sound of an explosion. He fell to the ground and was about to summon his water when he realized what had happened; there were a few burnt men on the ground. "Was that really the best way to handle that?"

"What did you want me to do?" Barrett asked him. "I ran into some people I couldn't see, knew they were wantin' to kill us, and I killed them."

"'Couldn't see'?" Eric asked.

"They're wearing the invisible clothing, too," Peter noted. "We need to move faster now. They'll of course know we were here."

They picked up the pace, and multiple times Eric and Barrett almost tripped, but in a few minutes they reached a large stone structure that, Eric had to admit, did look like an awkwardly-shaped duck. Peter took a device out from under his clothes and set it on a protrusion that had the appearance of a webbed foot, and he led the way back toward the shore, knocking on the first few trees so Eric and Barrett would know the general direction he was going. They heard gunshots again; it sounded like automatic weapons. Still they moved on.

"Why did we come back out here?" Barrett asked upon reaching the strand.

"Seemed easier than walking right into the depths of Riker's stronghold, no?" Peter responded.

"Fair enough," Barrett relented.

They heard more gunshots in the distance.

Aimee's face was covered in blood, but her eyes were determined. The men who had been randomly shooting had hit her, making her visible in the dim light. They seemed set on killing her, but Kandi knew they weren't confident they could. A tree off to Aimee's right suddenly began to sway before uprooting itself and flying in the direction of the combatants. It struck only one of them, and Kandi saw the tree fly back for another strike; but as the men ducked, the tree flew over them at the last second and straight at Aimee. Kandi immediately understood and used all her wind against the tree; it slowed, but had Aimee not been able to jump out of the way, she would've been killed. Guns started firing again, and Kandi recreated her wind shield around Aimee. The ground in front of Aimee rose into the air, and Kandi blew out the dust into the group of terrorists, momentarily blinding them. Aimee then compacted the dirt still in the air into a layer hard as rock and sent it flying. A bolt of lightning struck the earth, sending fragments back at the girls, and a large fire blazed behind them. Kandi took the oxygen away from the flame, essentially smothering it, and Aimee opened a hole in the island under where the shooters were standing. They were held out of the hole by a great wind before the earth literally reached up and swallowed them. Another bolt of lightning shot down, which Aimee blocked by bending the top of a still-rooted tree into its path. They both knelt, breathless.

"How well can you see me?" Aimee asked Kandi, still panting.

"If you stay in the shadows, it's hard. Are you okay?"

Grimacing, Aimee pulled her shirt up to show Kandi her wound for the first time. It was bleeding profusely.

"We need to find Mr. Talladega right now," Kandi told her.

"No, we can keep going." Aimee said through gritted teeth. She began to take off her shirt to tie it around her side to clot the blood, but Kandi stopped her.

"Don't take your shirt off! I'm not visible—here's mine." Kandi came into existence for a brief moment while working her way out of the shirt under her invisibility clothing before vanishing again. She handed her shirt to Aimee.

"Thanks." Aimee's breathing hadn't returned to normal.

"Are you sure you're okay to keep going?" Kandi asked her, concerned.

"I'm sure that I *will* keep going either way."

"Riker's apparently not too concerned with us right now, and he still almost killed us. Don't do something stupid just to look brave."

"I'm not," Aimee retorted. "This is how I've lived: you fight through pain to do what you have to do. Right now, we need to make sure none of these soldiers are left by the time Riker hits us with his remaining troops."

Aimee's sentence was punctuated by a gunshot and a scream from Kandi; Aimee went down, and Kandi looked for her attackers but saw no one. More gunshots rang out in Kandi's general direction, and she upended the trees near where she thought the shots were originating. Male screams rang out and she saw a few bodies appear under the fallen trunks. Alarmed at the realization of what was happening, Kandi grabbed Aimee's still body with wind and ran back to Dega and Dru, bringing Aimee along just under the canopy so she wouldn't be seen.

As she neared the clearing, Kandi saw a small light in the

distance. She recognized it as Dru's and went toward it. Dega's voice sounded a few seconds later. "Where's Aimee?"

Kandi let her down gently to the ground. "They're invisible, too, Mr. Talladega."

Dega breathed as if to say something, but then refrained. Kandi looked at Aimee and with horror realized she had been shot in the head. She saw Dega take the cloth away from Aimee's side and heal her there, but her head wound remained unchanged and she still lay lifeless. It hadn't hit Kandi until that moment that Aimee was dead.

"I'm sorry for being in your head," Dega spoke to her, "but for today it's important that I know what you guys are seeing. Aimee's not dead; I've healed her heart enough to keep her body going for a few days. My power can't penetrate her skull to reach her brain, though, so she needs to have surgery soon to have any chance of making it."

Kandi was dumbstruck. "Will she ever be normal again?"

"If I'm there when they operate, then yeah. The problem will be fighting Riker without her."

"You're sure there's no way to bring her back while we're here?"

"I'm not; I just know that I can't do it right now; let's get her back to the sub."

"How?"

"Eric's here."

They returned to the place where Dru was shining her hand as a signal. "Is Aimee okay?" Barrett asked worriedly when he first saw her.

"No," Dega told him, "but if she gets surgery she should be."

"Surgery?" Eric said in disbelief. "Are you sayin' you can't heal her?"

"I can't get through her skull to her brain."

"Is that the only problem?" Peter's voice asked.

Dega realized his mistake. "It's hard keeping up with multiple people at once, so I was just focusing on Kandi's mind and Eric's mind; I didn't even think to check you."

"What is it?" Dru's voice asked.

"I know how to help with that," Peter told her. "I would need a sterile place—"

"Do it here," Dega cut him off. "Nothing will happen to her."

Peter listed the tools he'd need, and Eric went to the sub to get makeshift ones. While he was gone, Dega yelled, "Look out!"

Dru set a ring of fire around the approached group of men, engulfing them in flames.

"Dru," Dega started, "you and Barrett go make sure no one comes near us while we're doing this. Listen for footsteps since we can't trust our eyes."

"If Dru's not here, how will I see?" Peter asked.

"By the moon," Dega told him. "Unless you kill her, I can heal anything you accidentally do to her."

In the thirty minutes following Eric's return, the circle of people around Peter and Aimee had to defend themselves against numerous attacks from Riker; he had realized what was happening and was determined to take advantage of their vulnerability.

When Kandi thought she would die of exasperation if Peter took any longer, she finally heard his voice. "I opened her skull."

"Hold her shoulders down. Eric, hold her ankles." Dega didn't say anything else, but after a few terse minutes Aimee opened her eyes and Peter had to restrain her so Dega could finish repairing her skull and skin.

"Aimee!" Kandi yelled when Dega was finished, throwing her arms around her.

"Hey, Kandi," Aimee said wearily. "I would hug you back but I can't see you."

Kandi laughed and Aimee heard the sound of her stepping back.

"Here," Eric's voice said, and out of nowhere appeared another set of the invisible clothing.

"Now what?" Aimee asked them.

Dega answered. "Now we wait for Dru and Barrett to get back before we demolish this island."

Gunshots punctuated his sentence, followed by an explosion and screams. No one but Aimee jumped, as Barrett and Dru using their powers against their attackers had been the norm for the past half-hour; however, the simultaneous mega-blasts that followed noticeably worried even Dega. Escaping the island was going to be hard for the Destined, as troops were converging upon the place where they had made their entrance on the island. Before Dega could suggest they do anything, though, unseen noises darted out of the woods. "We can't hold Riker off," Barrett's voice said. "Are y'all about done with Aimee?"

"Yeah, I'm fine," she told him. "Riker's actually here again?"

"I wouldn't call it *again*," Dega told her. "We've fought him before, but never so close; he's always been a long way off."

"Then how has he still managed to counter us?" Eric asked.

The wind picked up around them and seemed to whisper the phrase *Because I am that much stronger than you.* It was a warm wind, which Kandi thought was odd. It reminded her of being near the fireplace at Christmas time, just laying there with her family, growing drowsier ... and drowsier—

"*Push the heat away, Dru!*" Dega yelled. Slowly but surely Eric felt the wind return to normal temperature. He thought some of the others might have been burned, so he decided to mimic Riker and try to mix his water with the wind. Water droplets from the ocean moved into the air current, and he heard a sigh of relief from Aimee.

The forest in front of them suddenly burst into flames, and Eric would have quenched it had he not noticed it going away from them and toward their foe. The wind picked up behind it and pushed it along, and Riker was quiet long enough that for a moment Eric thought him dead. Then the flame suddenly diminished, and the entire might of the ocean came crashing from the other side of the island, the flame and the Destined in its path. Eric quickly tried pushing it aside; that worked to an extent, but a huge amount of water was still hurtling toward them.

Barrett, hoping that Riker was in contact with the water, shot a few bolts into it. The waves immediately lost the force of Riker's power pushing them forward, but inertia could not be hindered. Suddenly, Aimee conjured a rock in between Barrett's eyes and the water, creating a barrier that split the water and gave them a circle of about a fifteen-yard radius in the middle of the torrent.

Then the rocks imploded, throwing debris toward the Destined before anyone had time to stop it. Peter yelled out in pain, and Aimee fell to the ground, a scream held on her tongue. Dega was right next to Peter, who was now visible, and he healed him quickly before running to Aimee. Multiple times, lightning struck the path between Aimee and Peter until Eric created a semicircle of a shield of water with a small stream to the ocean. Barrett shot more lightning bolts into the woods.

Dega got to Aimee, who cringed every time she moved. She pointed to the side where she had been shot an hour earlier. Dega pulled her shirt up to see the wound and was relieved to find that there was no rock inside her. He healed her quickly, and she nodded and stood up. Dega took hold of her wrist and pulled her arm up straight so that it was pointing into the trees.

She understood and tried to make some of the trees in that direction fall but was unable to do more than sway them. She felt Dega leave her side and knew he assumed that Riker had stopped her. She didn't try to throw rocks because she knew she didn't have the strength for it.

"How do we fight someone if we don't know where he is?" Eric yelled over the commotion.

"Did you see Aimee sway the trees a second ago?" Dega asked him.

A lightning bolt shot toward Aimee; Barrett deflected it.

"No," Eric yelled, "I was too busy trying not to die!"

"Do it again, Aimee!" Dega called to her. She knew that it might be too much for her, but she did as she was asked and had to keep herself from falling.

"That direction from Aimee, about two hundred fifty yards into the trees!" Dega yelled to Eric.

Every drop of water from the ocean that was anywhere close to Eric stilled and iced over. It raised and reformed itself into a cone and went hurtling in the direction Dega had given him. A second after it disappeared, he saw a flash and realized there were shards in the air above them. "Kandi, blow the air above us back into the ocean!" He unfroze most of the shards, and a strong wind came and took them back to their original positions, the ocean already having made up for the decrease in volume.

The sand beneath their feet gave way suddenly, and Kandi had to pick everyone up and throw them into the place where water had flowed a few seconds earlier. A large fire shot through the woods, burning the trees on the outskirts that still remained. Kandi and Dru were able to control it for the most part, but the first few bolts that were shot through the fire hit their marks. Barrett didn't realize what was happening until he was hit and didn't go down. While Dega healed the shock from Peter and Eric, Barrett yelled out, "Your own power can't hurt you!"

"You serious?" Eric asked over the noise.

Barrett nodded.

His word was all that was needed. Immediately Eric threw himself in front of the ice hurtling toward Dega; the force of it made him fall, but he rose quickly, unscathed, lifted the ice, and threw it toward the fire, which it doused. Lightning rained down, being willed to cover a large area, but Barrett summoned it to himself; it came into contact with him and vanished from existence. He shot into what was left of the woods and heard an explosion.

"Why can he not absorb our powers?" Eric asked, looking at Dega.

In lieu of trying to reply over the noise, Dega's eyes got wide, and he shrugged and shook his head.

Trees flew seemingly out of nowhere. They all instinctively knew that Aimee absorbing the force of that would be different and could harm her, so Dru burned the trees and Kandi pushed them out of the way. Aimee tried to help but to no avail.

Fire came again, and Dru this time pulled it to her. As it was vanishing, she felt the power of it inside her. She released the newfound energy toward Riker in what was such a strong burst of power that everything else stopped; no one could bear to look as the blast left her.

It was so strong that Aimee felt herself strengthen at the very presence of another power so fully revealed. She stood straight and saw and thought clearly. Time slowed for her. She knew the blast was moving in the direction of Riker, that Riker might be able to stop it, and that it couldn't be allowed to happen. The island began to shake, all the way down to the very base. So violent had Aimee been able to make it that Eric and

Barrett fell, Dega had to catch himself, and Kandi had to use the air to steady herself. What few troops remained neither stood nor lay on the ground but rather were tossed about. Dru was still concentrating, engulfed in the power she had just released, and felt the flame hit Riker. Then the shaking was done, the brightness was gone, and Riker was quiet.

For a moment the seven of them sat there, breathless; only when a few shots rang out did they realize that they still had a job to do. They sprinted to the ocean and began swimming for the sub, which Eric was bringing closer to them. Shots kept ringing out, but none came close to them until one hit Peter in the head. Dega immediately realized what had happened and tried to heal him, but the wound was too severe; a few seconds more and Peter was dead.

They climbed aboard the craft without further incident. "Where's Peter?" Aimee asked; their suits had been cut enough from the fighting that they all had been made visible by then.

Dega's expression answered her question well enough. "There'll be plenty of time to memorialize Peter after we finish this," he said. He quickly moved to the weapons.

"Wait," Aimee said quickly.

Dega stopped, and everyone eyed her strangely. As tears appeared in her eyes they realized her hesitancy: Trevor. "You know it has to be done," Dega told her softly.

"Yeah, I know ..."

Kandi and Barrett both moved to her. "You're not alone anymore," Kandi said to her as she embraced her. "We're your family and we love you."

Aimee allowed the embrace and quieted herself.

Dega let her have another minute before he turned back to the controls. Peter had preprogrammed the computer with the coordinates of the locations where the bombs were placed, so

Dega only had to enter the command for *fire* for the missiles to leave the submarine in a flash of fire. Dega—and Eric with his water—guided the craft quickly away from the island. They felt six explosions, always the missile followed by the bomb. They resurfaced to see that the island was gone. The empty space weighed heavily upon them because of what they had had to do.

"So are we finished?" Dru said to anyone who would venture an answer.

"We're done with fighting," Dega told her.

"We're headin' back to the U.S. now, right?" Eric asked him.

"Yeah." Dega sighed, showing the extent to which he was struggling inwardly with a thought.

"Peter?" Kandi asked.

Dega chanced a glance at his body but had to look away. "No, he was a good guy, and I know where he lived in California. We can set up a tombstone for him there if his family is still alive, so I'm not worried about that. The fact that everybody still has their powers is making me think, though ..."

"Oh, I'd figured it was so Eric would be able to get us home," Barrett offered.

"No," Dega told him, "that doesn't take a lot of strength; he could get us back without the rest of us having it ... In the old books, occasionally the Destined were asked to set the world back to order again, but that was only the first few times they appeared, back when there weren't an excessive amount of people and civilization was still young."

"This war really hasn't been like any of them in the past, though, has it?" Kandi asked. "Not with all the technology. What if a new trend is starting?"

Dega shook his head and sighed again. "That has to be it."

"Wait, we can't go home?" Dru asked.

"We can go and stay a little while," Dega told her, "but we're not completely done."

"Earth is *really* big," Aimee put in, trying to keep her voice steady.

"Don't be so negative!" Eric told her, laughing softly. "We'll figure somethin' out. And as long as we ain't got Riker to worry with, I think we're good."

Aimee conceded the point and managed a smile.